The Truth

Erin McCauley

AUTHOR OF *THE CONFESSION*

CRIMSON
ROMANCE
F+W Media, Inc.

Published by
Crimson Romance
an imprint of F+W Media, Inc.
10151 Carver Road, Suite 200
Blue Ash, Ohio 45242

www.crimsonromance.com

Acknowledgments

I am so grateful for all of the love and support I'm constantly surrounded by. Thanks to Tammy Smith, for cracking the whip, holding my hand, and for continuously being by my side whenever I need you. Thanks to Diane Shaver, for all your input, words of wisdom, and hours of reading the same things again and again. Thanks to Diana Ballew, for being the perfect writing companion, and for your constant guidance. I love you all.

I am surrounded by the best friends a girl could ask for. To them, and they know who they are, thank you from the bottom of my heart for everything. I know each of you will find a part of yourself in Lexie, Marissa, Aimee or Emily. It is because of you I am able to write about true friendship.

As always, a special thank you to my family, for their support, love, and continued understanding of this crazy new, but wonderful, schedule. Your mother loves you very much.

Chapter 1

Lexie Wayne looked down at the tombstone and fought back the tears as Ryan bent down to place the bouquet of daisies on his mother's grave. The rain fell as if the sky wept for them. She adjusted the umbrella to shield them from the pelting drops.

"Do you think she sees us?" Ryan looked into her eyes as only an inquisitive four-year-old can.

"I think so, yes." She laid her arm across his shoulders in comfort.

"How come she left?" he asked, not for the first time.

"It wasn't her choice, Ryan. If she could have stayed with you forever, she would have." Looking into his innocent face, her eyes pooled with tears.

"But why?"

"God needed her with him, and He knew you and I would be okay, just the two of us," she answered, unable to contain the tears now rolling down her cheeks.

"How come he needed her?"

She searched for the words to explain the unexplainable. "Your mother was so special that God needed her to be a big angel and watch over a lot of people, instead of a mommy to look over only a few."

"So why are you only a mommy and not an angel? You're special, right?"

She ruffled his dark curls. "I'm not quite ready for that big of a responsibility. Besides, I believe you and I were meant to be together. Everything happens for a reason, even if we don't understand why."

"What's res- respons-?"

Lexie smiled, crouched down, and pulled him onto her lap. "Responsibility? Well, it means taking care of something big, something important."

Ryan narrowed his eyes, his lips pursed in thought. "So, God didn't need you to be an angel, but he needed you to be my mommy?"

"Exactly." Her heart swelled and she pulled him closer to her.

"I'm glad." He snuggled into her. "I'm glad you're my mommy."

She held onto him for a minute, closed her eyes, and basked in the feeling of his warm breath against her chest, and the comfort of his small arms wrapped around her. Placing a kiss on his temple, she stared at the tombstone of her friend. "Me, too, baby. Me, too."

Lexie had met his mother, Maggie, when she'd come to work for her at the coffee shop. They became fast friends and Lexie was the one to check her into Nathan's Hope Hospice House when her cancer had become untreatable. She had succumbed to the disease three years ago. Maggie would have been twenty-eight years old today, the same age Lexie turned just last month. She felt a tear slide down her cheek at the unfairness of it all. Lexie still missed her, but the life she'd discovered since moving Ryan into her home had become all-encompassing.

They stood in silence for a moment as the rain continued to fall, then Lexie took Ryan's hand and they began to walk across the grass. Lured by another gravesite beneath a large palm tree, she felt compelled to stop. Pulled forward by a force she hadn't felt in years, she knelt and gently ran her hand over the top of the smooth granite, now glistening with water.

"Your favorite kind of day," she smiled wistfully as she spoke to the stone. "Wet, but warm, with a strong chance of a rainbow."

"Who are you talking to?" Ryan knelt alongside her.

She straightened and pulled him to his feet. "An old friend," she managed to say, forcing the words through her constricted throat.

"Is your friend an angel like my mommy?"

Squeezing his hand, Lexie nodded her head as the tears ran down her cheeks. "One of the most important angels of all. He always was." She took a deep breath and blew it out slowly through pursed lips, and wiped the tears from her cheeks.

Turning to her son, she felt her love for him surge through her. "You want to go to work with me today?"

He grinned and nodded his head so fast it caused him to lose his balance. "Can I wear an apron, too?"

"Absolutely," she said. Locking away her sorrow, she forced a smile to her lips. "You must be in uniform if you're going to be serving the customers."

Tugging her hand, he dragged her across the grass toward the car.

Ryan bounced in his seat, unable to contain his excitement as they pulled into the parking lot outside of Lexie's coffee shop, Ocean Breeze Java. The car was barely in park when Ryan spotted his uncle through the window and tugged off his seatbelt before wrestling with the door handle. Ryan landed with a splash in a large puddle in his haste to get out of the car, chanting "Uncle Jordan, Uncle Jordan!" as he ran toward the shop.

Lexie rushed around the car and caught Ryan's hand, pulling him onto the sidewalk before another car whipped into the open parking spot beside them. Escaping her grasp, he scampered ahead of her.

"Ryan, slow down, wait for me!" She fumbled with the key, struggling to lock the car before she rushed after him. "Ryan, come here."

Ignoring her call, Ryan raced around the man who held open the coffee shop's glass door. Thrown off balance by the boy zipping past him, the man twisted, struggling to maintain his footing.

Foreseeing the disaster about to happen, Lexie grabbed for the door in an attempt to stop it from slamming into the man. The strap of her purse slipped from her shoulder and spilled its contents on the cement.

Like a slow-motion scene in a bad comedy, Lexie's left foot

came down hard on a tube of lip gloss and shot out from under her. She pin-wheeled her arms and struggled to regain her footing, resembling an amateur log roller. Unable to catch her balance, she latched onto the only thing close enough to grab—the already off-balance man in the doorway.

Pulling him down with her, the weight of his body slammed her to the sidewalk causing cartoon stars to whirl about her head and all the air to explode from her lungs in a large whoosh. She blinked her eyes and tried to get them to focus. She was currently seeing three and four identical things, all in different distortions.

She regained focus and looked up into intense green eyes, with the longest black eyelashes she'd ever seen. Skimming down, her eyes followed the path of a small bump on an otherwise straight nose splattered with a light trace of freckles. Strong cheekbones supported a shadow of dark whiskers. She felt the heat rise on her cheeks as her eyes fixated on his mouth and the smirk on his perfectly sculpted face.

Attempting to rise on her elbows, she realized he was lying across the entire length of her body, supporting his weight on one elbow like a lover basking in the afterglow.

Humiliated, she frowned and cocked her head. "Do you mind?"

"Not at all," he said, as the dimples in his cheeks deepened.

He placed his hands on the ground on either side of her head and lowered his face directly above hers. Her heart pounded in anticipation, her mind lost all thought, and she ran her tongue across her lips. But in one quick motion, he pushed off his arms and landed on his feet. With a mischievous grin, he held his hand out to her. "Here, let me help you."

Lexie felt her cheeks flush in embarrassment as she pictured how foolish she must look. She glared up at him and, ignoring his outstretched hand, sat up and picked up the contents of her purse. Determined to save what was left of her dignity, she stood, straightened her shirt, brushed off her knees like she was wearing

Gucci instead of old jeans, and ran her hand through her hair. She pulled her shoulders back and stuck her chin out in defiance.

Stepping around the insolent man, Lexie came face to face with her brother, Jordan, who stood watching the scene with uncontained amusement. Beside him, Ryan stood in silence with his head hung low, gripping his uncle's hand.

"Sorry, Mommy," he whispered to the floor.

"This wasn't exactly the introduction I had in mind when I brought him over here," Jordan said, biting back a laugh, "but Lexie, I'd like you to meet my new partner, Deputy Grayson Hunter."

Lexie turned around and locked eyes with the man, who was still wearing a self-satisfied grin, and groaned. "Perfect," she mumbled, "just perfect."

"Grayson, I see you've met my sister, Lexie. And this little speed demon is my nephew, Ryan."

Lexie clenched her teeth together. She wanted nothing more than to wipe the smirk from Grayson Hunter's handsome, chiseled face. Her body still hummed from the anticipation of his almost-kiss. Her hands itched to trace the lines of his face, to bury them in his thick black hair. She didn't like it. What she liked less was that her response had been noticed. Grayson's eyes shone with the spark of challenge.

She clasped her hands together, smiled sweetly, and batted her eyes mockingly. "New partner? Oh, that's such good news. The only thing missing from this town is a cop who's light on his feet and as graceful as a one-legged tap dancer."

Jordan groaned.

Grayson's eyes flashed with mischief. "You can't blame a man for being swept off his feet by a beautiful woman."

"Should we worry when he's swept off his feet by a four-year-old boy?" Lexie challenged.

Grayson ignored her retort, and held out his hand to Ryan. "It's nice to meet you."

Ryan giggled and reached out to shake the outstretched hand.

He stepped through the door behind a laughing Jordan and turned around, his eyes filled with amusement. "And Lexie, it was *very* nice bumping into you."

Chapter 2

Grayson shot upright, the covers pooling around his waist, his face masked in sweat. His chest felt tight. Opening his mouth, he inhaled, dragging air into his lungs. He could still smell the blood, hear the explosions, feel the sand blow across his cheeks and burn his eyes.

The nightmare replayed each night when he tried to sleep. A broken record of the death and fear he'd lived with for two years as a soldier, fighting in the deserts of Iraq.

The price he'd paid to become a soldier had been high. Everything changed the day he'd packed his duffle bag. The road he'd been on, the life he'd seen himself living, was a stark contrast to the reality he lived now. He'd never imagined he'd be waking up alone, shaking from a nightmare that wouldn't end, without her beside him to hold onto.

Looking around the room, he felt displaced. It wasn't a tent filled with cots and footlockers, and it wasn't his quiet little house nestled along the creek in Kentucky, just a mile from his family home. He'd needed a change, a fresh start. His parents had been hurt by his decision to move so far away. He understood their disappointment. They'd spent every day for two years wondering if he'd make it back. But after six months struggling to adjust to being home, he realized part of what he so desperately needed was to break away from them.

Grayson stepped from the bed and walked through the empty living room of his apartment. Having started his new job right away, he'd had no time for furniture shopping in the weeks since he'd moved in. He pulled open the shades and gazed out the window. The stars shone clearly in the California sky. It wasn't the smog-filled nights he'd pictured when he accepted the job offer in Carmel.

He didn't know why he'd chosen to come here. This was where she'd wanted to come, a place he'd never even once contemplated.

Still, when he'd seen the job opportunity he jumped at the chance. He wondered if he was a glutton for punishment.

His mind wandered to the spunky brunette he'd met earlier. Not met, really, more like crashed into. What a contrast she was to her brother, his new partner. She was sparks and fire where Jordan was calm and cool. She was outspoken and feisty, quick witted and exciting, all wrapped in a tiny, sexy package.

He recalled the way her amber eyes roamed, taking in every detail of his face. He'd been wrong the minute he decided to lean in close enough for a kiss, but he'd liked the information it gave him. She would have let him kiss her. The flash in her eyes, and the way she stood so tall when she couldn't have been more than five foot two, made him want to know more.

Maybe she was just what he needed. If he were to be honest, this was the first time in years any woman had caught his attention.

Stepping away from the window, he knew he wouldn't be able to go back to sleep, so he opened a box and began to unpack. He unloaded a box of glasses, placing them into the cupboard closest to the fridge. His new kitchen wasn't big, but it was conveniently designed, with frosted glass cupboards, dark cherry wood, granite countertops, and stainless steel appliances. There was just enough counter space to indulge his love for cooking, and possibly entertain the spunky pixie who continued to enter his thoughts.

Looking around, he couldn't bring himself to continue with the monotonous task of unpacking any more boxes. He needed to move, to escape the demons that threatened to overwhelm him. Decision made, he laced up his sneakers, grabbed his keys, and headed to the beach.

The sun had just begun to rise, creating splashes of orange, purple, and red that stretched out across the water. The waves rolled softly and created a soothing sound on the mostly deserted beach. Picking up his pace, his shoes dug into the sand, producing the resistance he enjoyed.

He inhaled the salty air, and pushed himself forward, trying to concentrate on the sounds of the seagulls, dogs barking in the distance, and the rumbling of the surf. Anything to erase the overwhelming feeling of loss, regret, and loneliness he'd awoken to.

The sun was above the horizon, now, and looking at his watch, Grayson realized he'd been running for over an hour and it was time to turn around. He still needed to shower and grab some coffee before his shift. The thought of coffee brought a smile to his lips. If he hurried, he could make it back in time to stop at Ocean Breeze Java.

Thinking again of the fiery woman who owned the coffee shop, he wondered if stopping for coffee each morning might become his new favorite habit.

Chapter 3

Lexie was crabby. She'd started her morning by stubbing her toe on an abandoned Tonka truck, pouring a half glass of left over apple juice down the front of her new shirt, and wasting fifteen minutes searching for her keys. She finally found them in the cargo hold of her son's favorite military airplane, parked beneath his bed.

Behind schedule and short staffed, she knew it was going to be a long day. Pausing as she walked through the door, she took a moment to appreciate the business she'd built. Small round tables were sprinkled throughout the room, surrounded by round-backed wooden chairs. Sage colored wing-back chairs were set in corners, separated by glass-topped wicker tables, inviting her customers to sit and stay a while. Small vases sat on tables, their fresh flowers splashing color throughout the room. Sunlight filtered in through the floor to ceiling windows that surrounded over half of the store. The counter boasted a brightly lit bakery display of fresh scones, cookies, and homemade rhubarb pie.

She tied her apron behind her back and headed for the kitchen to start a batch of blueberry muffins. The bell over the door chimed, announcing her first customer. She looked up with a smile, and her stomach flipped when she looked into Grayson's green eyes.

"Morning." The purr in his voice shot electricity through her system.

"Deputy Hunter, you're up early. Aren't I a lucky girl you've decided you enjoy my coffee." She replied, sarcasm dripping off each word. She wanted him to leave, to never have come at all, anything to stop her body from reacting to him with this uncomfortable yearning.

"It's not just your coffee I enjoy. But after a restless night, I could definitely use some."

Biting her tongue to stop her smart retort she simply said, "What can I get for you?"

"A large black coffee and dinner with you tomorrow night."

Her stomach lurched, and her heart rate increased. "One large black coffee coming right up." She turned her back to him in hopes of hiding the strong reaction she was having to him.

"And dinner?"

Determined not to let "yes" slip from her mouth, she decided to say nothing. What was it about him that made her want to run as fast as she could in the other direction? It was more than her not wanting a relationship, she'd never struggled to say "no" in the past. It was more than her embarrassment at having her attraction to him so blatantly exposed as she lay on the cement outside her shop the day they met. It was even more than the conflict going on between her body and her mind. She didn't want to want him. It was as simple as that.

She slid the cup across the counter. "It's on the house." She wanted to get him out of her shop as fast as possible.

Without looking away from her, he ignored his coffee and said, "You don't eat dinner? Or you don't eat dinner with men you've just met?" He cocked his head to the side, looking as if her answer would be so profound he was afraid to miss one word.

"I don't date," she said matter-of-fact, looking him directly in the eyes, willing him to give up his pursuit.

Dimples indented his cheeks and his eyes lit with challenge. "You'll take those words back before long. I have a way of breaking people down. It's part of what makes me good at my job." He winked at her, slid a couple of bills across the counter and strutted out of the shop.

He showed up the following morning, and the next three mornings, each time ordering a large black coffee, smiling at her, charming her, complimenting her, and each time asked her to dinner. Each time she declined. Each time it became more difficult; her body seemed to have a mind of its own.

Saturday morning she found herself watching the door for him, and was actually disappointed when he didn't show up. What was happening to her? She was sure she must be losing her mind. She'd made one promise to herself, and only one: she would never again allow herself to go through the pain love could bring. Her life would be filled with her family, her business, and her son. That would be all she'd need. It was the key to her happiness.

For eight years, she hadn't once questioned her decision not to date. Now, a week after bumping into Grayson—literally—she was daydreaming about the arrogant, handsome cop with a quick smile and the ability to make her body hum simply by being in the same room. His arrogance made her crazy. The fact he could see her reaction to him made her angry. The way his lips moved, the sparkle in his eyes, and the dimples in his cheeks when he smirked made her knees weak. He was costing her sleep, and that made her…well, that made her doubt her ability to keep him away, and that just made her angry all over again.

"Excuse me?"

Lexie shook her head, snapping herself back to reality as her eyes focused on the customer waving his hand in front of her face. The heat crept up her cheeks and she tried to force a polite smile onto her face. She could strangle Grayson Hunter right now. "Sorry, what can I get you?"

After the man had left, she grabbed a towel and walked around the counter to bus the tables. Her mind must have wandered again, because she was startled when she locked onto the smug, violet eyes of her best friend. Marissa sat silently, smiling in that irritatingly knowing way of hers, and sipping from a cup of coffee Lexie didn't remember pouring.

Lexie wrung the towel in her hands, searching for something to say to ease the tension she was feeling, and to erase the look from Marissa's face. She could think of nothing.

"I'll be damned. You are human." Marissa broke out laughing.

"What's that supposed to mean?" Lexie set the towel on the table, and plopped down into the empty chair.

"For as long as I've known you, I've wondered," Marissa stifled another laugh by quickly taking a sip from her coffee. "You were the only woman I knew who wanted nothing to do with men, but wasn't gay. It wasn't normal. Nobody human could keep that going forever. Now, here you are." She shook her head, her eyes lit with amusement. "Who is he?"

Lexie, breathing fast, shot out of her chair and began to wipe the table with vigor. "I don't know what you're talking about." Looking up at the door, she willed it open. Of course, as luck would have it, no one walked through the door to save her from her relentless friend.

"Come on, tell me." Marissa slid forward on her chair and leaned her forearms on the table.

"No." Lexie shook her head. "No. I don't know what you're talking about. There is no guy. No." She could hear the tone of her voice rising. "I'm tired that's all."

She inhaled deeply when the bell over the door offered her an escape. Turning to greet her salvation, she froze. Her hands fell to her sides, the rag falling slowly to the floor, her knees weak.

"Hey, Lexie. You didn't think I'd forgotten about you, I hope." Grayson stood there in a tight black t-shirt and snug jeans accentuating his tall frame and broad chest.

She didn't think it was possible for him to look any better out of his uniform, but he did. Swallowing hard, she struggled to find her voice. "Grayson," she finally managed.

Lexie whipped her head around when Marissa mumbled an all knowing, "mmm…"

Glaring at her friend, Lexie turned and headed for the counter, "The usual?"

Grayson sauntered over to the counter and leaned casually toward her. "No, today I want something icy. And dinner with you tonight."

"How about an Italian soda?" she offered, ignoring his second request.

"Or a nice glass of cold chardonnay over dinner," he prompted.

"I can't," was all she could manage. It was hard not to picture a relaxing night, sitting across from a charismatic man, sipping a glass of wine and leaving her fears in the past. Her skin tingled at the thought.

Grayson's face grew serious. "Lexie, why won't you have dinner with me? Are you afraid of men? Or is it you're afraid of me?"

Her face heated and she mumbled, "No, of course not!" She simply couldn't have dinner with him. But she also couldn't explain why. She was having a hard time remembering herself. "I have a son. I don't have childcare, especially with such short notice."

"Lexie, I have Ryan tonight, remember?" Marissa walked up to the counter, and eyed Lexie, all but daring her to weasel out of it. She smiled at Grayson. "I'm Marissa Neil, Lexie's friend. And you are?"

Grayson grasped her outstretched hand. "Grayson, Grayson Hunter. It's nice to meet you."

"It's nice to meet you as well," Marissa purred.

Lexie felt her chest tighten as she watched the exchange. Now what? If he didn't make her so flustered, she'd have been able to come up with a better excuse. But then, if her friend would've butted out, she would have gotten away with it.

Marissa leaned across the counter and whispered, "No guy, huh?" She smirked, and raised her voice adding, "I'll pick up Ryan from daycare, so you don't need to worry about a thing, Lex. Have a good time." She winked at Lexie over her shoulder as she left the shop.

Grayson turned to her, "I'll see you at six."

Lexie could only stare after him as he followed Marissa out of the shop. Crap.

Chapter 4

Fastening the last button on her blouse, Lexie tugged on the hem, straightening the soft blue silk over her short black skirt. Turning in a slow circle, she checked her reflection in the mirror. She really didn't know why she cared so much about how she looked.

The doorbell rang, and with one final glance at herself, she slipped on her strappy black heels and headed for the door.

Grayson whistled softly as his eyes roamed from her head to her toes. "You look amazing."

So did he. He wore a light gray sweater that accented his broad shoulders and trim waist over a simple pair of blue jeans. His eyes were bright, and his hair was tousled from the wind, giving him a carefree look.

She stepped back to let him enter, and all but salivated as the manly scent of his light cologne permeated her senses. "I thought we were going out?" she asked, surprised to see him holding a bottle of wine and a paper take-out bag.

"I decided I didn't want to share you, so I brought dinner." He walked past her and into the kitchen, setting the bag on the counter like he'd lived there all his life.

She turned to watch him as he opened one cupboard, then another before pulling out two wine glasses and then opened a drawer, searching for a corkscrew. A part of her wanted to be angry at him for his assertiveness, but she couldn't deny the fact that his self-assurance was alluring. His refusal to give up his pursuit of her should've bordered on disturbing, yet somehow it wasn't. It was charming and flattering. She wasn't sure how to fight against his advances; she only knew she had to. She was a mother now, and her life was no longer her own. She couldn't afford to make careless choices. A sweet-talking, gets-what-he-wants police officer was asking for trouble.

She hopped up onto the counter, watching as he unloaded Chinese cartons from the bag.

Glancing over at her, he set the last carton on the counter and smiled. "I couldn't figure out if you didn't like me, didn't like men, or if you had an embarrassing habit of dribbling on yourself when you ate and therefore weren't comfortable eating out in public."

She smothered her laugh, and accepted the glass he handed her.

"I decided the only way to know for sure was to spend a little time alone with you and, at the same time, watch you eat. Besides, who can resist Mongolian beef and eggrolls?"

The spicy aroma rose from the cartons as he opened them. Mongolian beef was her favorite.

"I don't dribble on myself." He smiled and handed her a carton and a set of chopsticks. Picking up her glass, she slid off the counter and headed toward the living room, slipping her shoes off and tipping her head in a beckon to follow.

The living room was bright and inviting. Homey was the look she'd been going for when she'd brought Ryan home. A wall of windows looked out over the ocean, reflecting the subtle oranges and reds in the sky at the beginning stages of the setting sun. She curled into the corner of the comfortable red couch, crossed her legs beneath her, and dug her chopsticks into the carton. Grayson sat on the other end of the couch, and silently watched her as he bit into an eggroll.

The intensity of his gaze made her uneasy. He gave her the impression he could read her mind. She'd never considered herself timid or shy, especially around men, but he made her nervous. All of her self-assurance seemed to leave her when he was around. The wall she'd built around her didn't feel high enough or strong enough to keep him out. She didn't like the fact he affected her in that way.

"Go get changed." The tone of his voice made the simple order sound like a soft caress.

She shook her head, attempting to break the invisible rope

pulling her to him. "What's wrong with what I'm wearing?" Her voice resembled a petulant child, and not the grown, nobody-tells-me-what-to-do woman she was.

"I want to walk on the beach, hold your hand, and watch the sunset on the water."

She opened her mouth to reply, but no sound came out. He sat watching her. His mouth twitched in one corner making it obvious he knew the affect he was having on her. He made her feel powerless over her own emotions. She didn't like it. "Unless you're afraid you won't be able to control yourself," he challenged, his eyes full of mischief.

She snarled, hoping it sounded more like the "not a chance" dismissal she intended, and less of the "I don't know what to say to that" sound she heard. She stood up and took a large swallow of her wine. "There will be no hand holding. We're not on a date. I agreed to have a meal with you, for the simple purpose of getting you to stop asking."

This time, his face broke into a wide smile, and he winked at her.

"I am only agreeing to take a walk with you because it will get you off of my couch and closer to your car." She stood up and walked from the room, the sound of his amused laughter followed her until she closed her bedroom door with a snap. She leaned against it and took a couple of deep breaths.

She needed to place some distance between them. Her body threatened to demolish the last shred of self-preservation she had. Every part of her wanted to melt into him. She couldn't recall ever wanting a man more. She also knew Grayson was the type of man who could snap a woman's heart into little pieces, especially hers. She needed to be smart. Her heart wasn't available and never would be. It was fragile, not strong enough to stand another heartbreak. He was sexy, cocky, and wore a badge. Three major strikes against him.

Lexie pulled on her jeans along with a pale peach sweater, and took one last deep breath for strength before walking into the living room. To her surprise, he'd put the food away, washed the glasses, wiped her counters, and corked the wine. "You didn't have to do that. I could have taken care of it later."

"It was a few cartons and two glasses." He tilted his head and creased his brow. "Exactly how long has it been since you've had a man in your life, Lexie?"

"I…I…" She felt the color rise on her cheeks. "It's none of your business. And what does that have to do with anything?" she snapped, relieved to have found her voice.

Ignoring her questions, he grabbed his keys, and handed hers to her. "Ready?"

*

Grayson watched her as she walked a foot or two ahead of him. Her sandals dangled from her fingers by their straps, her bare feet catching the waves as they rolled onto the beach.

She was a complicated woman. He knew she was attracted to him. No matter what her mouth said, her body language and her eyes told him the truth. What he didn't understand was why she continued to keep him at arm's length. He wanted to get to know her, but she shot him down on every attempt.

He assumed she'd been hurt in the past. Was it by Ryan's father? He'd tried to get Jordan to fill in some of the blanks but he'd only say the story with Lexie and Ryan was complicated, and she'd tell him herself when, and if, she was ready.

Regardless of her past, he wanted a piece of her future. No matter how small. She'd made him come alive again after years of barely existing. A weight lifted from him the minute he'd looked into her surprised eyes. Now, all he had to do was convince her to let him in. He was beginning to think his only way in was by pushing and shoving. He could do that.

Picking up his pace, he caught up with her, and reached over to grab hold of her hand. As he'd assumed, she instantly began to tug her hand away, trying to break his grip. She stopped and turned to face him, her other hand on her hip, her lips pursed.

They stood in a silent challenge with each other while the waves lapped at their ankles. His heart began to race. Her eyes grew wide. He took a step closer to her. She took a step back, inhaling a breath. He reached out and pulled her against him, her arms automatically coming to rest on his chest, her sandals leaving particles of sand on his shirt. He wasn't sure if her intent was to be closer, or to push him away. He lifted his hands and ran them through her hair, never taking his eyes from hers.

Her expressive eyes showed uncertainty, confusion, and longing. Using gentle pressure against the back of her head, he kept her from bolting. Her eyes fluttered closed and her body gave up its fight, growing soft in his arms. He gently brushed his lips over hers, taking his time, exploring their shape and texture. Parting her lips, he deepened the kiss, his tongue stroking hers. A soft moan escaped her lips and shot through his system like electricity. Gripping her tighter, he suckled her bottom lip and nibbled it with his teeth. Dropping her sandals, she reached over his shoulders and dug her hands into his hair, pulling him closer, taking her fill.

With reluctance, he loosened his grip on her, and pulled away. He watched her as her eyelids fluttered open. Their eyes locked. She stepped back, looking as if she might run. He took hold of her hand and started walking down the beach.

He had been longing to do that, but now that he'd touched her he wanted to take her in his arms again. Judging by her nervous behavior, he decided it might be best to slow it down and give her time to realize he was nowhere near done kissing her.

Chapter 5

In the weeks that followed, Grayson had integrated himself into her life. All of her good intentions to keep him at arm's length failed miserably. How was she supposed to fight a man who turned her brain to mush when he kissed her? Making him harder to resist, he not only made her happy, but her son as well. Somehow, Grayson had slipped into her son's life like he'd always been there. He shared his love for the stars with Ryan and the two of them spent hours laying on the beach, with Grayson pointing out the constellations, and telling Ryan the stories behind their names.

It was a beautiful Sunday afternoon, and the three of them had decided to spend the day in San Francisco. Lexie lifted her hand and waved at Ryan as he whizzed past her in his shiny red bumper car. The sound of his laughter rang through the air as he slammed into the side of Grayson's car. Grayson mumbled something about getting even, and hit the gas, chasing after Ryan and trying to cut in front of him. She heard her son's moan of disappointment as his car came to a stop, followed by an explosion of giggles as Grayson scooped him up and threw him over his shoulder, tickling his side as they headed toward her.

"Can we go again?" Ryan asked her breathlessly once he had his feet back under him.

Grayson stepped over and wrapped his arm around Lexie as he answered her son. "How about we eat first? I'm starving."

"Then we can go again?" Ryan grabbed ahold of Grayson's free hand.

"We'll see," Lexie responded, prompting a groan from Ryan.

As they drew closer to Fisherman's Wharf, Ryan raced ahead, enthralled by the large metal crab statue. "Come on, Grayson, come on," he urged.

"Hang on buddy, we're coming. Slow down," Grayson called after him, pulling Lexie along with him.

As Ryan picked up speed, ignoring his calls, Grayson ran after him, and grabbing him around the waist, hoisted Ryan onto his shoulders. Lexie felt her chest constrict at the comfortable picture they painted.

They stopped at the railing and pointed out the large sea lions sunning themselves on the docks below. Walking farther down the pier, Grayson pointed out Alcatraz across the water and explained its history to them.

An older couple walking past stopped and smiled at the animated little boy. "Your son seems to be enjoying himself," the woman said to Grayson.

Grayson smiled and nodded his head as they walked by, neither correcting her nor confirming her assumption.

Ryan giggled. "Grayson, she thought you were my daddy."

Grayson tilted his head and looked over his shoulder. "She sure did. But she doesn't know that any son of mine would never try to kill me with a bumper car."

Ryan erupted with laughter again. "Yuh-huh he would, 'cause you can't drive it."

As the two of them debated back and forth which one held the best bumper car skills, she couldn't miss the questions written on Grayson's face when he looked over at her.

They hadn't talked about Ryan's parentage. She wasn't even sure if he knew Ryan had been adopted. She hadn't been in a relationship since becoming his mother, and she'd never had to clarify to anyone. Ryan was her son, and how that came to be wasn't necessarily in the forefront of her mind. But this was different. Grayson was different.

"Ready to eat?" Grayson asked her.

Nodding her head, she took the hand he offered and walked through the open door into the Crab House on Pier 39. They took a seat and placed their order. Lexie reached over and tied the plastic bib around Ryan's neck.

"I'm not a baby!" he snapped, trying to rip the bib from his neck.

Grayson tied his own bib around his neck. "No, you're not a baby. If you were, you wouldn't be able to crack your own crab like the grown-ups."

Ryan straightened his bib, suddenly appearing proud to be wearing it. He looked over at his mother and broke into laughter again. "Mom, you look funny."

"Me? What about you two?" Lexie asked while struggling to look hurt by his comment. She couldn't do it. She laughed as she looked down at herself and across the table at Grayson.

When their lunch arrived, Lexie showed Ryan how to work the cracker, and use the small fork to remove the meat. He wore more than he ate, but his determination to do it himself melted her heart.

After four more rides on the bumper cars, and a double feature of *Toy Story* and *Toy Story 2*, Grayson carried an exhausted Ryan into his room. Lexie managed to get him out of his dirty clothes and into his pajamas before he fell asleep.

Closing his bedroom door, she walked into the living room and curled up on the couch beside Grayson and leaned her head on his shoulder. He kissed her forehead, and asked, "Are you tired?" He pressed his cheek against her head and ran his hands through her hair.

"You two wear me out." She snuggled closer to him, enjoying the sensation of his fingers in her hair.

He lifted his head and turning toward her, reached out and gently raised her chin. "I've wanted to do this all day," he told her before pressing his lips to hers. Her body melted into him, drawing the kiss deeper.

Breathless, she sighed with pleasure and wiggled herself into the crook of his arm, happier than she could have imagined. "I think Ryan had a great day."

"I think you're right." He spoke softly, his voice soothing her. "There's something special about seeing the world through the eyes of a four-year-old. But I think I had the most fun."

Grayson was talking about the day, his voice like a lullaby in her ear. She tried to concentrate on his words, but her eyelids were heavy and she struggled to keep them open. He mentioned the woman who'd thought Ryan was his son, and asked her a question she didn't hear as she drifted off to sleep.

Chapter 6

"When's Grayson coming?" Ryan threw himself onto her bed. "Mom, when? I've been waiting, but he's not here. When's he gonna be here? All our stars are out!"

She sat on the edge of the bed beside him, and frowned when she noticed the anticipation in his eyes. "Ryan, you're going to spend the evening with Grandma. Tonight, Mom is going out with Grayson alone."

"Why can't I go? Am I in trouble?" His eyes welled with tears as he sat beside her, swinging his feet over the edge of the bed.

"No, sweetie, you're not in trouble." Placing her fingers beneath his chin, she tilted his face to hers. "It's just that sometimes grown-ups need to spend time alone, to talk about adult stuff."

"I can plug my ears." He stuck out his bottom lip, his eyes pleading with her.

"There will be other times, but tonight, Mom needs some time with Grayson, alone."

"That's mean," he shouted, rushing from the room.

His bedroom door slammed. "Ryan!" she shouted, heading to his room.

The doorbell interrupted the scene, and Lexie sighed as she walked to answer the door. She smiled at her mother as she breezed in, asking for her grandson.

"He's in his room, throwing a tantrum." She sighed. "He doesn't understand why he can't go with us tonight."

"He has sure gotten attached quickly," Betty said, hanging her purse over the back of the stool in the kitchen. "Does that worry you?"

"It does." She sat down in the stool and looked at her mother. "This is all happening so fast. I never believed I would meet somebody again, let alone somebody who was so incredible with Ryan."

Her mother slid onto the stool beside her. "You really like him, don't you?"

She bowed her head, nodding. "I really do, and I'm scared to death he's going to break my heart."

"It's already too late, baby girl. You're a goner." Her mother patted her knee. "Now let me go see if I can console my grandson."

Lexie sat at the counter and watched her disappear into Ryan's room. Her mother was right, she was a goner. He'd somehow slipped into her life, and wrapped himself around her heart.

The doorbell rang, but before she could get off of the stool, Ryan flew out of his room, and threw open the door. "Grayson," he screeched, wrapping himself around his legs.

"Hey, buddy." He smiled, and reached down to pull him into his arms. "Think you can help me with this?"

His eyes grew wide as he looked over Grayson's shoulder. Ryan pushed out of his arms, and she could hear his deep intake of breath when he stepped around him.

They came through the door carrying a large telescope between them. "What in the world?" she managed to utter.

"It's a star watcher." Ryan said with excitement. "It's to see the cop-stale-ache-ns."

Grayson laughed. "Yes, it is to see the constellations. I don't think your grandma knows the stars like you do. I thought maybe you could show her Cassiopeia."

Ryan followed closely behind him as Grayson sat the telescope on the deck. He bent over and peered into the eyepiece showing Ryan how to work the focus. Ryan ran back inside, and rushed out again, dragging his bathroom stool behind him.

Betty walked over to Lexie as they both took in the activity on the porch. "And you said it would never happen again." Her mother threw her arm over her shoulder and gently squeezed.

"It's different now. I'm a grown woman and know how much pain comes from loving someone who doesn't stay. It's even worse now that I have Ryan to worry about."

"It's not the same, Lexie. History doesn't repeat itself like that.

What happened to you was horrible, tragic, and heart wrenching, but very different. I think you're looking for signs that aren't there, and being unfair to Grayson and yourself in the process."

"I don't think I'm looking for signs. I think I'm just trying to be smart. At least as smart as I can be when my heart is working against me." She turned and looked at her mother, searching for understanding. "Mom, this is the rest of my life we're talking about, and Ryan's. I have to be careful…"

"I think you're in big trouble if you're not ready for the rest of your life. I think it's already here. Don't let your fear dictate your future." She reached out and gently caressed her daughter's cheek. A twinkle of mischief flashed in her eyes. "Besides, Ryan and I are both ready for you to settle down, and we both think he could be the one." Betty winked.

A half an hour later, Lexie sat across from Grayson at her favorite seafood restaurant on the water. She couldn't silence her mother's words. Was this really it? Was he the one? Why did the thought terrify her as much as it excited her?

She looked around, touched he'd taken the time to find out her favorite restaurant and request a table by the window so they could watch the sunset. He continued to surprise her. Each passing day seemed better than the last. So why was she so reluctant to just let go?

"What are you thinking so hard about?" he asked, interrupting her thoughts. "Your face is all scrunched up, and you're biting your lip in that nervous way of yours."

Her hand rose to her lips. "I do not bite my lips, and I'm not nervous." They both knew she was lying.

"So next you're going to tell me you weren't thinking of anything at all, right?"

"Ryan is really attached to you," she blurted.

"And I'm really attached to him." He took her hand in his, lightly brushing his thumb over her knuckles. "Does that bother you?"

"No…yes…" She looked up, surprised by the concern she saw in his eyes. "It doesn't bother me as much as worry me a little. I don't think he's ever grown attached to someone so quickly before. I don't want him to get hurt."

His eyes grew serious. "I wouldn't hurt him. Even if you get tired of me and decide this date will be our last, I'd like to believe we'd remain friends, and that you would allow me to spend time with Ryan on occasion."

She felt a warmness race through her, an unfamiliar longing that wrapped around her heart and squeezed. She took a deep breath and tried to force herself to tell him what she was feeling. "I don't want tonight to be our last date. Ryan isn't the only one who's grown attached to you in a short period of time."

He brought her hand to his lips and gently kissed her palm. "I didn't believe this would ever happen for me again. I'm very glad it did."

They were interrupted when the waiter arrived with their dinners. Setting her napkin in her lap, Lexie picked up her fork and pulled off a flake of her salmon. She moaned her approval. His eyebrow raised and the corners of his mouth twitched. "I sure like the way you enjoy food."

She broke off another bite and fed him across the table. He closed his eyes and moaned as well.

"You're right, it's delicious."

As they ate, Lexie finally asked the question nagging her since they were interrupted. "You mentioned that you didn't think this would happen *again*? Do you want to tell me about the first time?"

Grayson's eyes grew dark. He didn't speak for a few moments, and she was beginning to wonder if he didn't want to tell her about his past. "I've never really talked about this to anyone," he finally said, his eyes appearing to search for something she couldn't see. "Saying it out loud makes it seem foolish that I haven't."

Lexie remained silent as he appeared to struggle for words.

"I met a girl when I was on leave in New York. She was a dancer. Young, carefree, and full of life. I fell hard, I thought she did, too. I was stationed in Washington State at the time, and after only five days together, she came back with me." He paused, almost like he was waiting for her to react. Finally, he asked her, "Does that seem crazy to you? That you could get so caught up in someone so quickly?"

She shook her head. If he would have asked her that before meeting him, she would have said it was beyond crazy, even foolish. Now she knew how quickly you could fall.

"We were happy. At least I believed we were. We talked about getting married, starting a family." He cleared his throat. "When I received orders to Iraq, we even talked about getting married before I left, but she didn't see any reason to rush it. I didn't see any flags, not one. The morning before I deployed, she walked into the barracks, and told me it was over. Just like that, no explanation, just see you later, goodbye. I never heard from her again."

Lexie could see the pain in his eyes. The confusion was still evident in the tone of his voice, the hurt still raw beneath the surface. "It must be hard…the not knowing why part." He nodded his head. "Did you ever try to find her?"

"When I was in Iraq, I wrote to her. Trying to understand, wishing she would explain. I never heard back from her." He reached over and grasped her hand. "It was a long time ago. I'm glad I'm here now."

She could see he genuinely meant it. She squeezed his hand in reassurance. Her heart ached for him, and in that moment, she knew she would do anything she could to chase the hurt from his heart.

"What about you?" He asked, still gently stroking her hand on the table.

"What about me?"

"Do you want to tell me about Ryan's father, or is that subject off limits?" His eyes were comforting.

"I know very little about Ryan's father." She smiled when his brow creased in confusion. "I adopted Ryan when his mother passed three years ago. All I knew of his father was that he had died before Ryan was born."

He stuttered. "I didn't realize…I just assumed…"

"Of course you did. Why wouldn't you?" She smiled at his astonished expression.

Finding his voice, he asked, "Has there ever been anyone? Anyone special, I mean."

Her heart clenched and she looked down at the table to break his gaze while she tried to control her reaction. It had been close to eight years, but the pain was still fresh each time she remembered. "There was, but it was a long time ago."

When he didn't speak, she looked up. He silently watched her, waiting for her to continue. She wasn't sure what to say.

"You loved him?"

She nodded her head, fighting back the tears. She knew if she spoke, her voice would crack and the dam would break.

"Lexie?" His eyes were filled with compassion.

"I don't think I can do this tonight. I don't want to do this tonight." Her eyes pleaded with him to understand. "There have been too many bad memories discussed for one night, and I, for one, want tonight to be a good memory."

"Okay, if you're not ready…" He said reassuringly. "But you will tell me about him, won't you?"

She squeezed his hand. "I promise, but for tonight, how about we get out of here, and really enjoy our alone time?"

Grayson's hand shot up in the air. "Check please."

Chapter 7

Lexie looked around Grayson's living room. It was filled with boxes and there was almost no furniture with the exception of an old desk, a couch, and the large bed she could see through the open bedroom door.

"Can you tell I wasn't expecting company?" He asked, picking a stack of clothes off the floor and setting them onto a closed box.

She slipped off her heels and set them on top of the nearest box. "Haven't you lived here for a few months now?"

"Well, yeah, but I haven't been here much. I sleep, go to work, and then find some excuse to hang out with you."

He stepped over to her, and lifted her chin for a kiss. It was slow and gentle, and she felt it all the way down to her toes. She felt dizzy when he pulled back, and she placed her hand against his chest to brace herself.

"I may not have any furniture, but I bet I have a bottle of wine in the kitchen. Could I interest you in a glass?"

"Definitely."

She slid onto the kitchen counter and watched him. He rolled up the sleeves on his cream-colored linen shirt and she watched as the muscles in his arms as he worked the cork. Tearing her eyes away from his arms, she realized he was standing still, watching her as he held a wine glass in each hand. Heat crept up her cheeks, and she lowered her head.

"I don't think I'll ever get tired of you looking at me like that." He walked closer and stood in front of her. "I also love the way you blush when you realize I've caught you staring."

"I was not staring," she said defensively. "And I certainly wouldn't blush if I were. You have the largest ego I think I've ever encountered. How do you make it in the real world believing everyone is just panting in your wake?"

"Not everyone, just you." He stepped closer, using his body to stop her attempted escape as she slid off the counter. "And it's not ego, its fact. Knowing what you like is a good thing. Knowing that what you like is me is even better." His eyes locked onto hers. The earlier amusement that danced in their green depths changed to desire.

He tilted her head back and pressed his mouth to hers. Her body arched in an attempt to close the space between them. She wrapped her arms around his waist and pulled him to her. His lips lightly brushed over her cheek and down her neck. She tipped her head to the side, giving him easier access.

"You do have a big ego," she mumbled.

He nibbled on her ear lobe and whispered, "It's only going to get worse if you keep looking at me the way you do."

Her brain short-circuited as she grasped for something sarcastic to say in response. He brought his mouth back to hers and dug his hands into her hair. Her body caught fire as she struggled with the clothes that separated his flesh from hers.

She unbuttoned his shirt, slid it over his shoulders and down his back, letting it fall to the floor. She dropped her arms long enough to pull her own shirt over her head and unhook her bra. Wrapping her arms around his waist, she ran her hands softly over the rippled muscles along his back.

A moan erupted from her throat as his hands gently brushed her naked breast. Her nails dug into his back when he slowly rolled her nipple between his fingers. She fumbled with the buckle of his belt, wanting him more than she'd ever wanted anyone.

She stumbled when he suddenly stepped out of her grasp. His face was flush, and his breathing labored. He held up a finger, as he struggled to speak.

"B…Bed…we need to get to the bed." He walked over and lifted her into his arms, pulling her close against his chest. "Our first time can't be on the kitchen counter. That's more of a third or fourth time."

Cradled in his arms, she leaned in, running her tongue up

the length of his neck. He moaned, the vibration sending flashes through her body. Running her hands through the soft mat of dark hair on his chest, she slowly rolled his nipple between her fingers as he'd done to her.

"The floor is going to have to do if you don't stop for a second. We're almost there."

"I don't see what was wrong with the count—"

Her cell phone rang. They stood frozen in the center of the living room. She buried her head into the crook of his neck and willed it to stop. The ringing stopped, and both of them breathed a sigh of relief.

She smiled up at him and gently kissed him. He'd taken only one step forward when her phone rang again. This time, she pushed out of his arms and reached for her purse.

"I'm so sorry, it's my mother's ring tone, and she wouldn't call back if it wasn't important." Her hands shook as she pressed the connect button.

"Mom, what is it?"

"It's Ryan. I'm so sorry; I don't know how it happened. He fell and I can't stop the bleeding. We're on our way to the hospital. I'm sure he'll be fine, but I wanted you to know. I feel horrible."

Lexie reassured her mother before hanging up. She shoved her cell phone back into her purse and threw it over her shoulder.

"Grayson, I'm sorry, I have to go. It's Ryan. He's on his way to the hospital, and I have to get there."

Before she could finish her sentence, he'd gathered their clothes, tied his shoes, grabbed his keys, and was waiting by the open door.

"Hurry, Lexie."

Chapter 8

The minute they'd been cleared to enter the back hall of the emergency room, she spotted her mother walking toward them with Ryan in her arms.

She rushed forward, and her heart raced when he turned his tear-streaked face to her.

"Mommy." His voice hitched as he reached his arms out to her.

"Oh baby," she crooned, holding him close. "What happened? Are you okay?"

"I got stitched." His sadness faded and his face beamed with pride as he lifted his bangs to show her the bandaged spot on his temple. "It hurted, a lot, but I only cried a little."

"You're so brave," she kissed his cheek.

"What happened, buddy?" Grayson asked him, coming to stand beside her and investigating his bandage.

"I fell," Ryan said simply.

"He was looking through the telescope and his stool tipped over," Betty said. "He didn't fall far, but he caught the end of a nail sticking out of one of the rails on the porch. The nail was so small, I couldn't even find it at first, but he caught it just right." She brushed her hands over her grandson's hair. "There was so much blood I think it scared us both."

"It was a gusher," Ryan interjected.

"I bet it was." Lexie smiled. "I'm so glad you're okay, sweetie."

"I found the dipper," Ryan informed them, looking proudly at Grayson. "The big one."

"That's great. I think we'll need to pick you up a more stable stool for when you show it to me."

"Can I show you now?" Ryan leaned over and climbed onto Grayson, wrapping his arms around his neck.

"I think you should rest tonight. A battle wound like that one would have even the bravest soldier assigned to quarters for a day or two."

"Yeah," Ryan nodded his head in agreement. "I coulda bled to death."

Grayson chuckled. "It's a good thing Grandma was looking out for you."

Ryan nodded again. His serious expression had both women turning their heads to hide their smiles.

"All right, little man," Lexie said, reaching over to pull Ryan into her arms, "It's time to get you home and into bed."

Ryan twisted away from her, clinging tighter to Grayson. "Isn't Grayson coming too?"

Grayson looked over at Lexie and mouthed, "Please?"

She smiled, "Yes, Grayson is coming with us. But there will be no star gazing or play time, its right to bed, deal?"

"Deal," they both said in unison.

Lexie turned to her mother. "Go home and get some rest." Pulling her into her arms, she whispered into her ear, "He's fine. It was an accident, they happen all the time, remember? Stop looking like you were irresponsible or negligent."

Betty sniffed, and squeezed her daughter tighter. "I'll call in the morning and check on him. I'm so sorry."

"You're doing it again," Lexie scolded. "Now kiss your grandson goodnight, and get home to Daddy."

Betty stepped over and rubbed Ryan's back as he lay comfortably against Grayson's chest. Bending over to kiss his cheek, she whispered she loved him, waved at the three of them and headed out through the emergency room doors.

Grayson shifted Ryan to one arm, and held out his hand for Lexie's. "Ready?"

She nodded her head, took his hand, and let him lead her out to the car.

"Grayson, did you ever have to get stitched?" Ryan asked as Lexie settled him in the backseat.

"Yeah, I've had lots of stitches," Grayson answered.

"Did you have gushers, too?" Ryan asked.

"Yup, I've definitely had a gusher, that happens sometimes when you're a soldier."

Lexie realized she'd never asked Grayson much about his tour of duty in Iraq. She waited with interest for the answer as she buckled herself into the passenger seat.

"You ever get shot?" Ryan asked, his eyes filled with wonder.

"Actually, I have, yes."

"What? You never told me that," Lexie burst out, her stomach suddenly queasy.

Grayson shrugged. "Honestly, I try not to think about it too much."

"You got shot? Whoa! I bet that took a whole bunch of stiches," Ryan chimed in.

Grayson laughed. "You bet, buddy. I even got a scar out of the deal."

"Wow! Hey, Mom, do you think I'll have a scar?" he asked excitedly.

Lexie paled a bit at the thought. "I don't think so, sweetie. Your battle wound is not as bad as Grayson's."

Ryan harrumphed, and then turned to look out the window.

"Where did you get shot?" Lexie asked Grayson quietly.

He rubbed his left shoulder. "Shoulder. I got lucky, the bullet missed the bones. Hurt like a son of a gun, though."

"I didn't notice a scar," she said, thinking back to their earlier tryst when he had been shirtless.

"I believe you had other things on your mind," he said, a hint of playfulness in his voice. Lexie swatted at him affectionately, and he grinned.

Once they'd arrived home, Lexie tucked Ryan into the middle of her bed. He wanted to be close to her, and she knew she wouldn't be able to sleep with a wall separating them.

He'd insisted on a bedtime story and Grayson was currently propped up against her headboard, with his long legs stretched out over the comforter, reading *Green Eggs and Ham.* It was the type of scene that would melt any mother's heart, and she was no exception. Listening to the fluctuation of his voice as he spoke to Sam I Am and the sound of Ryan's giggle, her heart swelled.

Climbing in next to her son, Lexie let the sound of Grayson's voice lure her to sleep.

The following morning when she awoke, she looked over at her sleeping son and past him to the man sleeping soundly on the other side of her bed. He hadn't gone home. Instead he'd covered her with an afghan, turned off the lights, and slept beside them.

It wasn't the morning after she'd envisioned as they'd raced to his apartment last night, but she knew at that moment, that it was a morning after she'd never forget. It was the morning she fell in love.

Chapter 9

Grayson jumped in his seat when Jordan slammed a large pile of files onto his desk.

"Where were you, Hunter?"

Looking up into the curious face of his partner, he could feel the heat rise on his cheeks. He hadn't thought it would be a problem dating his partner's sister, but having just been interrupted recalling the softness of her skin as he'd run his hands over her naked flesh, he realized it had its uncomfortable moments.

"Sorry, just thinking. What's up?" he asked, trying to pull himself back to work.

"Whatever you were thinking must have been good." Jordan chuckled and plopped down in the empty chair beside the desk. "How'd it go last night?"

Grayson replayed last night in his mind. It had been perfect, really. The way her eyes drifted closed when he kissed her, the way her body arched against his hands when he touched her. He knew he was falling for Lexie. He'd started the minute he'd laid eyes on her. But waking up this morning, watching her sleep with one arm resting gently across her son, he knew it was no longer falling. He'd fallen—hard.

"It wasn't what I'd expected, but it went well, I think." Grayson shrugged his shoulders nonchalantly.

Jordan's eyebrow rose. He leaned forward and braced his arms on his knees. "The look on your face told me it went much better than well. Let's forget it's my sister for a moment. I recognize that look. You don't have to talk to me about it, but don't pretend that I don't know either."

He wasn't exactly sure what Jordan knew, but he did know it wasn't easy to forget it was his sister at this moment. "Dinner was delicious. Conversation was easy. She looked beautiful. But our evening was interrupted when we had to go to the emergency room with Ryan."

"What?" Jordan shot out of the chair. "What happened? Why the hell didn't anyone call me?"

"He's fine, Jordan, really." Grayson rose from his chair and squeezed his shoulder reassuringly. "He fell and caught his temple on a nail of some sort. There were a few stitches, that's all, honest, he's fine."

Jordan took a deep breath and blew it out slowly. "Thank God. I don't know what I'd do if anything happened to that kid."

"I can understand that. I think I was as panicked as Lexie when Betty told us she was on her way to the emergency room with him. I don't think I've ever gotten dressed that fast before."

Jordan's eyes drew together, and his lips became a straight line, but he didn't say a word. In the silence, Grayson realized what he'd said and felt the heat rise on his face again.

"No...not...It wasn't like that. Well...shit, Jordan, nothing happened. Stop looking at me like that."

Jordan erupted with laughter. "You should see your face. It's priceless."

Grayson sat down in his chair, and pulled a file off the top of the stack on his desk. What he really wanted to do was knock the amusement off of his partner's face.

Jordan cleared his throat in an apparent attempt to get his laughter under control. "Sorry, man, but you have to admit that was funny."

Grayson turned and glared at him and said nothing.

"So I take it my nephew's accident interrupted your plans for the evening."

Grayson's fist clenched. He didn't really know why, but he really wanted to punch him. He leaned in closer to Jordan. Glaring at him he spat, "First of all, it wasn't my *plan* for the evening. Having a night alone wasn't a premeditated attempt to sleep with her. And second, Ryan needing his mother was not an interruption in my book, it was reality. She's not some fling, and I understand who comes first in her life. I'm more than fine with that."

Jordan sat in silence with a serious expression on his face. Finally, his mouth twitched at the sides then broke into a huge grin. He slapped his hand against his thigh and hollered, "I'll be damned. I was right. You're in love with her."

Grayson knew his mouth was hanging open, but he seemed incapable of closing it. Was he that transparent? His palms grew sweaty and he tried desperately to get a denial to cross his lips. He wanted to tell Lexie how he felt before her brother blurted it out over coffee.

The radio went off, saving him from further embarrassment. "Robbery in progress at 18421 Canal Street, suspect is armed. Possible hostage situation."

Jordan responded to the call as they raced from the office.

They pulled up in silence. No sirens or flashing lights until they could evaluate the situation. There was one other car on the scene, and both officers were anxiously waiting Jordan's arrival.

"What've we got?" Jordan asked, scanning the surroundings.

"As far as we can tell, there's one gunman and two possible hostages inside. No demands have been made, and the phone inside has gone unanswered."

Three additional patrol cars pulled in, all flagging the entrance. Jordan motioned the men and all took cover behind their car doors and drew their weapons as he reached for the bullhorn.

Before he could speak, the doors were thrown open and the suspect came out holding a gun to the head of a young store clerk. She was screaming and crying, begging him to release her as he clung tightly to her neck.

Judging by the way his hands shook and how his eyes struggled to stay focused, Grayson knew he was strung out. The kid was nineteen, maybe twenty, and high enough to shoot before thinking.

"Put down your weapon and release the hostage." Jordan spoke with authority into the bullhorn. "We don't want anyone to get hurt."

Removing his gun from the side of her head, the suspect pointed at the police officers and shook it back and forth. "Back up man, you're too close. Back up or I'll shoot her." He screamed, saliva spitting from his mouth, his eyes flicking from one officer to the other.

"You don't want to shoot her, son. Put down your weapon and we can try to work something out. Nobody needs to get hurt here."

While Jordan tried to hold his attention, three of the officers made their way to the back of the building.

Grayson inhaled a deep breath, trying to stifle the sounds of automatic gunfire and the screams of brave men from his mind. He hadn't been on the other end of a barrel since being shot in Iraq. He'd been sure he was ready for anything then. Knowing the life of the young store clerk and his partner were both in his hands, he hoped he was ready now. Wiping his hand on his thigh, he tightened the grip on his gun.

Suddenly, everything began to move in fast forward. The suspect threw the store clerk to the ground and aimed his weapon at Jordan. The door blew open and another gunman came through, shooting round after round in the direction of the officers.

Jordan stood and shot at the first gunman, hitting him in the shoulder and causing him to drop his weapon, but the second gunman now had a clear shot. Grayson rushed from behind his cover, jumped in front of Jordan and pulled the trigger.

He watched the suspect hit the ground before everything went black.

Chapter 10

Lexie felt like she was walking through fog. Nothing was clear, her thoughts weren't making any sense, and her emotions were running close to the surface. She'd been so sure she'd never love again. That it wasn't possible after the loss and heartbreak in her past. They were still strangers in a lot of ways. She didn't know anything about his family, where he grew up, why he'd joined the military or why he'd gotten out. She didn't know his favorite color, although she'd bet money it was blue. She didn't know if he was allergic to anything or if he still had his tonsils. As she went through her normal routine, she found herself questioning the feelings that surged through her.

She had never been a woman to jump in head first. She was cautious, rational, a realist that didn't ever let her emotions take the lead. So why did she feel like her feet weren't connected to the ground? Why couldn't she catch her breath when she thought of her life without him?

"Lex, you okay?"

Looking up into the worried eyes of her best friend, she smiled, "I'm fine, sorry, making lists in my head." She hated that her first instinct had been to lie.

"Nice try. Spill it." Marissa sat on the edge of the desk and crossed her arms.

Lexie and Marissa had been friends since high school. Sometimes she hated that Marissa could read her so well, but it didn't surprise her after so many years. Marissa was the head nurse at Nathan's Hope Hospice, and after Ryan's mom had passed, Lexie became a volunteer one to two days a week as a way of giving back.

"I'm waiting," Marissa reminded her as she began to tap one tennis shoe impatiently against the floor.

"It's nothing, really…"

"It's definitely something. You are never distracted, and today I'm afraid to let you near the patients. You've got something on your mind, so out with it." Marissa slid further onto the desk.

"Ryan went to the emergency room last night."

Marissa's eyes grew wide. "Is he okay? Why are you here? You should be home with him."

Lexie reassured her worried friend. "He's fine, just needed a couple of stitches and Mom's with him. That's not it."

"Then what is?"

"I was with Grayson. He was so wonderful with Ryan. He even stayed the night to help me take care of him." Lexie blew out a frustrated breath.

"I don't understand. That sounds like a good thing, so why do you say it like it's not?"

Lexie ran her hand through her hair and shook her head. "I don't know if I'm ready for this. He's damn near perfect for me."

"He's perfect for you? He's wonderful to your son and treats you like a queen? He's sexy, funny, and employed? That bastard!" Marissa clenched her teeth and pounded her fist against the desk in mock anger.

Lexie cocked her head to the side and watched Marissa's performance. "I know I sound ridiculous. It's just that…it's just… these feelings scare me to death. He makes me laugh, he makes my knees weak when he kisses me, and Ryan is nuts about him. But there's so much at stake. He's the first man in a long time to make me feel anything, but there is still so much I don't know about him."

"We never know everything, Lexie. The discovery is part of the process."

"I know you're right. There is still so much I want to learn about him. So why am I freaking out?"

Marissa placed her hand gently on Lexie's shoulder. "Have you told him about Kyle?"

Lexie shook her head.

"Why haven't you?"

Lexie looked down at her hands folded in her lap. "I don't know. It never seems like the right time."

"Or maybe you're afraid he'll realize you compare him to Kyle every time he puts on his uniform."

Lexie's head shot up. "I do not." Her voice cracked. "I…I…I do not!"

"Yes, you do." Marissa nodded her head. "You know it and I know it. But it isn't fair to Grayson and you know that."

"I don't compare…exactly." The corners of Lexie's mouth trembled, and her voice lowered to barely a whisper, "I just remember."

"It's okay to remember." Marissa grasped both of Lexie's hands and squeezed. Looking directly into her eyes, she added, "But remember the happy memories, the love and the laughter. Don't hold so tightly to the end."

Lexie opened her mouth to speak and jumped when the phone rang beside her. She held up a finger urging Marissa to stay and picked up the receiver. "Good afternoon, Nathan's Hope."

There was a long pause on the other end before she heard someone clear their throat. "Lex, it's Jordan."

She immediately knew something was wrong as she held to phone to her ear.

His voice quivered. "You need to come down to the hospital."

She shot out of her chair, knocking it to the ground. "Is it Ryan? Is he okay?" She didn't think she could stand another scare like she'd had last night.

"Ryan's fine." The silence crackled through the phone line. "It's Grayson."

Her hands shook and tears ran unchecked down her cheeks, "Grayson?" She finally managed to ask.

"Lexie, he's been shot."

Chapter 11

Lexie struggled to catch her breath as she hurried down the hallway of the emergency room. Again. She stopped and leaned against the wooden rail that ran the length of the wall and squeezed her eyes shut, trying to block out the visions of blood and tubes flooding her thoughts. She couldn't do this again. She'd known that the minute she fell for Grayson. Why couldn't she find a nice doctor, or a lawyer to fall in love with, a successful man with a safe job? Anyone who didn't wear a badge or carry a gun.

Jordan stepped into the hallway, and, spotting her, made his way to her side. Concern was etched in his face as he pulled her into his arms. "He's going to be fine. He was wearing a vest so the bullet didn't enter his body. He's got a few broken ribs and a small concussion from landing on the cement, but he'll be fine." He smoothed her hair beneath his large hands, like one would a scared child and spoke to her in a soft tone. "He saved my life today. I'm just so glad he took the time to put on a vest."

She couldn't speak. Concentrating on the words Jordan was saying, she tried to erase the visions from the past. Nodding her head, she opened her mouth to respond. The lump in her throat burst in a small howling sound, and she began to sob. Her body shook as Jordan pulled her tighter against him, whispering encouraging words she couldn't understand.

"I can't do this," she finally managed to whisper.

"Can't do what, sis?" He didn't release his hold of her.

"I can't be in a relationship with a cop. I just can't go through this anymore." Her sobbing escalated, as she leaned in closer to his chest.

"That's not fair. Grayson is going to be fine. He's a smart cop. You can't punish the both of you because of the past." Jordan tipped her head back to look into her face. "You never told him, did you?"

She shook her head.

"Don't you think it's time you did?"

She didn't answer. Instead, she walked past him into the bathroom. She leaned against the sink and stared at herself in the mirror. Streaks of mascara ran the length of her cheeks. Her eyes were red and swollen, and the fear still lingered there. She needed to pull herself together and take the last few steps down the hall to Grayson's room. The worst part was she didn't know what she would do once she got there.

She turned on the faucet and splashed cold water on her face. Reaching for a paper towel, she scrubbed the make-up from her cheeks and beneath her eyes. Pulling out a compact, she attempted to cover the red blotches the remained on her face. It was obvious she'd been crying, but she also knew it would be a good hour before the evidence was gone, and she couldn't wait that long to see him.

She spotted Jordan leaning casually against the wall when she emerged from inside. She took a deep breath and asked, "Where is he?"

"I'll take you," he replied, reaching down and taking her hand. When they stopped outside the door to his room, he turned to her, "Don't do or say anything you'll regret. Take some time to think it through before you make any decisions, okay?"

She nodded her head and pushed open the door. Grayson appeared to be sleeping. The sheet lay at his waist, exposing the wrappings around his rib cage, and the scar on his shoulder where he'd been shot before. She noticed the large purple lump on his right temple, and the scrapes along his arm. She fought down the knot in her throat and walked around to the side of his bed. She sat quietly in the chair next to him and stared at the man who'd given her a second chance at love.

Every part of her wanted to run. She didn't want to feel the fear, the worry, or remember the endless pain. She couldn't even feel relieved that his injuries were so much less than they could have been. His eyes fluttered open and a smile covered his face when he spotted her.

"You look terrible. Stop worrying, I'm fine." His voice was thick and scratchy, evidence of the heavy doses of medication still running through his system.

Unable to speak, she reached over to take his hand.

"The clerk made it, Jordan's okay, and the bad guys are locked up. See, everything is fine. I'm fine." He squeezed her fingers running his thumb over the back of her hand.

She laid her cheek against the back of his hand and closed her eyes, trying to soak up the comfort he was desperately trying to give her. Her mind drifted back in time to the muffled shouts of doctors, the beeping of machines, and endless amounts of blood. She squeezed her eyes tightly, trying to block out the visions. She couldn't. She heard the panic escalate in the doctor's voices, the rushing of feet against the linoleum floor, and the sound of the heart monitor as it stopped beeping. Then the long horrible buzzing as the peaks on the heart monitor flattened into an endless straight line.

Panic threatened her again, as her chest constricted, and her eyes burned with the tears threatening to spill. She sat up in the chair and pulled her purse onto her shoulder before standing up. "I have to get Ryan, but I'll come see you tomorrow. Get some rest," she said, avoiding his eyes.

She could hear him speak but couldn't make out his words as she rushed from the hospital room, her face once again covered in tears.

Chapter 12

Grayson tossed and turned, unable to get comfortable in the small hospital bed. His mind continued to replay the scene from the day before. What had happened with Lexie? It didn't make sense. She'd rushed from his room without a backward glance, and now she wouldn't answer his phone calls. She seemed to be pushing him away, but why? He'd tried to talk to Jordan when he came by but he simply said Lexie had a hard time with hospitals. Jordan wouldn't look him in the eye when he spoke, proving to him it was much more than that, and nothing Jordan was going to divulge. How was he supposed to understand if she wouldn't even talk to him?

He would be discharged in the morning and had left a message asking Lexie to pick him up. He needed to see her and knew his anxiousness was keeping him awake, causing the time to go by incredibly slow. The night nurse came in to check his vitals, and scolded him for not resting. After she injected sleep medication into his IV line, he smiled gratefully at her and finally nodded off to sleep.

He awoke late that morning to something heavy landing on his bed. He struggled to focus, rubbing his eyes and scooting up on the bed. He scowled when he saw Jordan sitting on the end of the bed, his duffle bag on his lap.

"Where is Lexie?" Grayson snapped.

"She's not feeling well, she wanted to make sure you got home safely and called me to pick you up." Jordan rose and pulled his clothes out of the duffle bag. "I bet you'll be glad to get out of here."

Grayson recognized Jordan was uncomfortable and felt badly for him, but he couldn't just let it go. He didn't understand what he'd done to push her away. "That's a lie, Jordan, and not a very good one. Why is she avoiding me?"

Jordan helped him into his shirt, and set his boots on the floor. "You'll have to talk to her. I'm in the middle here and I don't like it."

"How can I talk to her if she won't even answer the damn phone?" His voice rose. "What the hell did I do?"

"You didn't do anything. Just give her some time, she'll come around." Jordan set the magazines stacked on the table into the bag and threw the bag over his shoulder. "Let's get you home."

Grayson stood up and obediently sat in the required wheelchair. He reached out and clasped Jordan's arm. "You and I both know I have no intention of going home. We can do this one of two ways: you can drop me off at Lexie's, or you can drop me off at home and I will immediately climb on my motorcycle and drive myself."

Jordan sighed and stepped behind the chair, wheeling Grayson slowly from the room, mumbling under his breath the entire way.

As Grayson knew he would, Jordan diligently dropped him off at Lexie's door, shook his head in disapproval and drove off, still chattering under his breath about stubbornness, life being unfair, moving to an island in the Caribbean, referencing the fact he would always be single, and how none of this was his fault but he'd be the one Lexie blamed.

Grayson stood outside her door, trying to decide how to start the conversation once she opened the door. His mind was blank. He'd just have to wing it. Taking a deep breath, he rang the doorbell. He waited a few minutes and rang it again. Nothing. Clenching his jaw and balling his fist, he painfully pounded on the door. "Lexie, open the damn door!"

The door remained closed, and no sound came from the other side. He knew she was home. He'd spotted her car when he arrived. This time he rang the bell, and pounded in intervals he knew made him sound crazy. He also knew he wasn't going home until she talked to him. "Lexie!" He shouted again.

He heard a small voice on the other side of the door, "Grayson, is that you?"

He hadn't realized he'd been holding his breath until his lungs released it in one large exhale. "Yeah, Ryan, it's me. Could you open the door and let me in?"

"Sounds like you, but how can I know for sure? Mom won't let me open the door without her."

"Pull up the stool in the entry and peek out the hole on the door. You will be able to see me." Grayson listened to the sound of the stool scraping on the wood floors and stepped over to stand in clear view of the peep hole.

"Hi, Grayson."

"Hi, buddy, can you unlock the door for me?"

Ryan opened the door and threw himself at Grayson, sending shooting pains throughout his body. "I heard you got shot. Can I see?"

"Easy buddy, you're a lot stronger than you were yesterday."

"Really?" Ryan crooked his little arm and making a fist, lifted his sleeve to check his bicep.

"So where's your mom?" Grayson asked, walking slowly toward the living room. His ribs ached, his head felt like it was going to explode, and he wasn't sure how much longer his legs were going to hold him up.

"She's in the shower. You wanna play video games with me?" Ryan plopped on the couch and swung a remote his way, elbowing Grayson in the side.

His eyes watered as a blaze of light flashed before them. "I'll just watch you play," he responded, his voice cracking with the effort.

When Lexie finally emerged from the bedroom, Ryan was deeply engaged in a race of Mario Kart and Grayson was resting his head against the back of the couch, holding his arms tightly to his chest, his forehead lightly covered in perspiration. He was in a lot of pain, and he realized that the smart thing would have been for him to go home and rest. But he had to talk to Lexie. Nothing was more important.

"Grayson, what are you doing here?" Lexie sounded both happy and anxious.

He watched her closely, filled with a mixture of curiosity and fear. Something wasn't right, and he was incredibly frustrated she didn't trust him enough to tell him what was wrong.

"Why didn't you come pick me up?" he asked her, never taking his eyes from hers. "I know you're not sick, and I also know you're avoiding me. What I don't know is why."

"Ryan, do you think you could go play Legos in your room so I can talk to Grayson in private?"

"Ah, Mom…after this race?" Ryan whined, never taking his gaze from the television screen.

"Now please." Her tone was stern, her meaning clear.

Ryan turned off the television and mumbled under his breath, as he walked to his room with his head hung down.

They both listened to his door close. Grayson didn't take his eyes off her. "What's going on, Lexie? Why do I get the feeling I'm not going to like what you have to tell me?"

Looking down, she took his hand and held it in hers. She traced an invisible path along the line of his knuckles. "You're an incredible man…" she began, as she tried to blink away the tears in her eyes, "but…"

"But what, Lexie?"

"I…I can't do this."

"Can't do what? Me? Us?" Grayson sat forward on the couch, his eyes still locked on hers, registering shock and a touch of anger.

"Yes…No…it's hard to explain." She looked down again. "It's because of…"

"Because of what? What's changed? Two days ago, we were fine." He slowly rose from the couch and began to pace. His moves were listless, his words slightly slurred, but he could feel himself starting to panic.

"It's not you, it's me." Her voice pleaded for understanding.

"That's B.S. and you know it." He spun around, physically flinching at the effort. "You and I have something here. So what changed in forty-eight hours? Is it Ryan? Because you know how much I care about him. You can see that can't you?"

"Ryan is crazy about you," she said. "It's not about Ryan, or you. It's me. I'm not ready for a relationship in my life right now." She wouldn't meet his gaze.

"You're a coward." He shook his head in disbelief, as he turned and walked out, slamming the door behind him.

Chapter 13

Jordan looked like he wished he were anywhere else but here. Grayson refused to feel bad; he hadn't called him. It was the nosey ass bartender who'd called him, and the guy should've just minded his own damn business. After all, he was a grown man; he could drink away his sorrows if he chose to. Granted, he hadn't taken into consideration the amount of pain medication he was on when he'd started on the Scotch, but he was still capable of getting his own cab.

"Come on Hunter, let me take you home." Jordan tried again to remove the glass from his fingers.

"I said—" Grayson hiccupped, "I said I got this." Downing the remaining contents in his glass, he slammed the glass to the counter and stood from his stool. The bar began to spin, and he could no longer see Jordan. Reaching for the bar to steady himself, he missed, bumped into the stool and sent it clattering to the floor. Hands beneath his arms steadied him as he hung tightly to the bars edge struggling to find his feet. He turned and looked into the eyes of his partner.

"Thanks, Wayne. Let me buy ya drink." Grayson attempted to set the stool upright and almost fell again.

"Not tonight, it's time to get you home." Jordan led him through the crowd toward the front door.

"Can you believe she dumped me?" Grayson swayed, and grabbed the jacket of a man passing by to hold himself up. The man turned around, causing Grayson to stumble again. Grayson hit the man's chest with a hard thud before stumbling backwards and craning his neck to look up into the man's angry face. "Just like that…done…finito…over."

The man reached down and grabbed Grayson by the shirt, lifting his feet off the ground. "Sounds like a personal problem," he spat. His eyes were slits, his cheeks twitched, evidence he was clenching his jaw, and he set Grayson back on his feet.

Grayson tried to straighten his shirt, knocking himself off balance again. He bumped into someone standing behind him, who in turn cursed, and shoved Grayson the opposite way, sending him crashing into the broad chest of the angry stranger. The man placed one hand on Grayson's shoulder, and forming a fist with his other, pulled his arm back.

Grayson squeezed his eyes closed, preparing for the impact. He slowly opened one eye and peeked at the man when nothing happened. Jordan had a hold on his arm.

"I don't think you really want to assault a police officer, especially in front of his partner." Jordan released the man's arm and stepped beside Grayson. "We were just leaving."

Heading for the door, Grayson stumbled again. "She won't even tell me why. She's a coward, that's why, and I told her so." Grayson stopped to brace himself against the doorjamb as he slowly lifted his foot to step outside. The light from the sun burned his eyes like hot coals, and the constant spinning of the world beneath his feet began to force the scotch back to the surface.

"Easy there, I've got you." Jordan wrapped his arm around Grayson's waist and led him to the passenger side of his truck.

When Grayson awoke in his bed, the sun was beginning to rise again to start the next day. His head pounded, his mouth felt like it was filled with cotton and his body ached. He threw back the covers, unsure how he'd gotten out of his boots and jeans, and made his way to the kitchen.

Running cold water into a large glass, he poured it down his dry throat before filling it again and swallowing some much needed pain medication. Taking the glass with him, he paused, noticing Jordan sprawled precariously on his couch.

He touched him on the shoulder. "Jordan, you don't have to stay here. I'm fine, and you don't look comfortable. Go on home and get some sleep."

Jordan slid up to a sitting position and rubbed his eyes. "How are you feeling? And what time is it?"

"I have no idea what time it is, and I feel like I lost a heavyweight fight with Rocky Balboa. Was I in a fight?" Grayson sat on the empty end of the couch and took another large drink of water. He hoped his bruised body would heal quickly, he was the best man at his friend Mark's wedding in a couple of weeks, and although Mark would get a laugh out of his current appearance, his bride-to-be would kill him.

"Yeah, you were. With a barstool and the barstool won." Jordan chuckled at the memory. "And please tell me you didn't really call Lex a coward yesterday."

"I did, and she is. She pulled out the 'it's not you it's me' card, tucked her tail between her legs and bailed. What else would you call it?" Grayson sighed in frustration. "It just doesn't make sense."

"Actually, it does." Jordan blew out a breath.

Grayson could tell he was struggling with something. "Jordan, if you know something, tell me. I know and appreciate your loyalty to her, but man, I can't lose her." He ran his hands over his face, and looked into Jordan's eyes. "Please."

"She should be the one telling you this. I told her she should, and now she's got me back in the damn middle." He shook his head. "Has she ever mentioned her past relationships?"

"No, not really, she listened to mine, but then changed the subject." Grayson braced himself, fearful that he would learn there was someone else.

Jordan continued. "In high school, she was in love with a boy named Kyle. He was a nice kid, they dated, well, forever it seemed. A couple of years after high school he proposed and she accepted. He was a rookie cop at the time, making a name for himself and working hard to build a solid foundation for them both." Jordan paused. "She really should be the one telling you this."

"I agree, but for whatever reason, she isn't, and if this is leading to why she's running from me, I would really like to understand."

"It was a week before the wedding, and Kyle responded to a domestic abuse call. The woman, girl actually, had been raped and beaten by her stepbrother, and was holding a gun to him and her own mother, who hadn't believed her when she'd told her what was happening behind closed doors."

"That's terrible." Grayson could imagine the scene. The girl's desperation, and her belief that she was out of options.

"Kyle was able to calm the situation, and had the girl safely out of the house. The boy had confessed at some point and Kyle had him cuffed and was leading him from the house. That was where it went bad." Jordan appeared to go back in time, reliving the scene as he talked.

"The mother, having learned the horrible things done to her daughter, snapped at some point, and pulled a gun of her own from a drawer. She shot at the boy, and killed him, but she also shot Kyle."

Grayson gasped.

"Kyle didn't live out the night, and Lexie was with him at the hospital when he died."

Grayson's stomach knotted, and his chest tightened. He leaned forward and placed his throbbing head in his hands, picturing the pain she'd endured.

"You're a police officer..."

"And I was just shot..."

Jordan nodded his head.

Grayson recalled the look on her face when she sat beside his hospital bed and his heart broke for the young girl who'd watched her fiancé die. Fear crept in when he realized his badge could cost him the woman he loved.

Chapter 14

It had been two weeks since Grayson walked out her front door. Two very long weeks. She knew it was for the best, but her heart wasn't as easily convinced. Making the situation more difficult was the fact he'd kept his word and made multiple requests to spend time with Ryan. Her son wasn't speaking to her for sending Grayson away, and his silent treatment was compounding heavily with the emptiness she felt.

Marissa had told her she was her own worst enemy. Jordan informed her she was making a huge mistake and mumbled something about letting the criminals win. He didn't understand. The fact he also wore a badge made it impossible for him.

She pushed the stack of napkins into their holder, and reached over for another stack when the bell above the door chimed. Her heart beat fast as she turned toward the door and she sighed when she saw it was Eva from the bank next door. She knew Grayson was going back to work today, and she hadn't realized how much she'd hoped he'd maintain his old routine. She didn't like the feeling of disappointment that overwhelmed her.

She faked a professional smile, and stepped behind the counter to get the teller's order.

"I heard about the shooting." Eva stated, pulling her wallet from her purse. "It wasn't your brother was it?"

"No, he's fine," she replied placing the lid on the tall vanilla latte. No, it wasn't her brother, it was simply the man she loved. "It was his partner, Deputy Hunter, but he's doing fine." She rang up Eva's purchase and handed her the change.

Eva's mouth opened like a sucker fish against the side of a fish tank. "Hey, isn't your brother's partner also your boyfriend?"

"No," Lexie answered in a dismissive tone.

Eva looked down at her cup and ran her finger slowly around the plastic lid. "I thought you two were seeing each other." Looking up, her cheeks turned red. "Do you think he would go out with me if I asked him?"

Lexie looked at the young, tall, curvy blonde with the kewpie mouth and large blue eyes and her stomach clenched. "I wouldn't know."

Eva leaned back as if she'd been struck. Lexie hadn't meant to snap at her, but the visual of Grayson with anyone else was painful. Eva nodded her head, lifted her hand in a silent wave and walked out of the shop.

Leaning against the counter, Lexie lowered her head, ashamed of the way she had behaved. How was she supposed to move on from Grayson when he was in her every thought? How was she supposed to smile and wave when he came by to pick up her son and she wasn't included? How was she going to be okay when every single, attractive female in town was competing for his affection? She ran her hands over her face, and expelled a breath before she attempted to lose herself in work.

The bell over the door rang again, and she smiled at the two beautiful blondes walking toward the counter. "What are you two doing here?" She asked, coming around to hug them both.

Aimee Morrison, one of her dearest friends, bobbed her head toward her mother, Emily Sinclair. "Mom can't seem to find the perfect something new."

Emily's eyes shone with the threat of tears. "She has no idea how important this day is to me. It has to be perfect. Your daughter only gets married once and I never thought I'd be there to witness it. So if we have to scale every shop to find the perfect thing, so be it." She tilted her chin in the air in mock defiance.

Aimee rolled her eyes. "If it doesn't happen soon, I'm afraid I'll be half way to New York the night of my bachelorette party."

"She's exaggerating." Emily shook her head, and looked disappointedly at her daughter, "We will barely be through Vegas as slow as she drives."

The three of them laughed and sat down at a table near the counter. Lexie couldn't help but feel the joy sparking between the two of them. It was hard to imagine it had only been a little over three years since they'd been reunited. Twenty-eight years earlier, Aimee had been kidnapped as a newborn, and it wasn't until the woman who'd taken her became ill and confessed her crime, that she'd finally found her mother. They looked so much alike, and were so comfortable with each other it was impossible to imagine them ever having been apart.

"We just left the Nathan Talbot House and Marissa told us what happened with Grayson." Emily reached out and patted Lexie's hand. "I hope you two work it out. Like I've told you before and you still refuse to hear, fear is simply the killer of dreams," she scolded.

"I know, I know." Lexie waved her hand hoping to dismiss the conversation.

Emily Sinclair had known Lexie for years and had never agreed with her decision to happily become an old maid. She was a wonderful woman, and a great friend. As the founder of the hospice house, named after her husband and Aimee's father, Nathan Talbot, she'd been instrumental in caring for Maggie, and at Lexie's side when she lost her. She was also the woman who'd rushed through the adoption paperwork so Ryan would never be taken to state custody, and was still actively involved in Ryan's life.

They discussed the wedding for a bit, and Aimee threatened Lexie's life if she missed her bachelorette party the following weekend. Her excitement was contagious and Lexie found herself questioning her decisions. After Ryan started his own life, she'd grow old alone. Was that really what she wanted?

As if reading her mind, Emily stood to leave, and wrapping her arms around Lexie's shoulders, whispered into her ear. "There is nothing in this world more necessary than love. Even knowing the outcome and the pain, I wouldn't trade one day with my Nathan.

Don't cheat yourself out of the happiness waiting for you."

Emily's words stuck with her long after the pair left the coffee shop, and eight hours later, Lexie stood outside of Grayson's apartment wringing her hands. She lifted her hand to knock and lowered it again. What was she going to say? She tried to play the conversation out in her mind, but each time she looked foolish, indecisive, and well, like a coward. She turned her back to the door and took a step to leave. She shook her head, took a deep breath and turning around, finally knocked on the door. This time, she refused to be a coward.

Instead of the anticipated look of surprise, Grayson looked as if he were expecting her. He smiled and opened the door for her to enter, stepping back out of her way. Her breath caught when she looked up at him. The bump on his forehead was gone and he wore a pair of baggy sweat pants with his chest bare of a shirt or any bandages. She could still make out a few purple areas but they didn't take away from the heated reaction she was currently having as she yearned to run her hands down his chest.

Color crept up her cheeks when she looked into his eyes and saw the flicker of knowledge in their depth. "I don't know why I'm here." Her tone conveyed her frustration.

He didn't say anything. He simply walked into the kitchen and poured her a glass of wine. Handing it to her, he sat quietly on the couch, waiting for her to continue.

She paced back and forth, sipping from her glass. The silence weighed heavily in the room as she tried to understand why she'd come. Letting out a sigh, she placed her glass on the coffee table and turned to leave. "I shouldn't have come." Her chest felt tight, her breathing rapid as she gripped the doorknob.

"I'm glad you did. I've missed you." Grayson said, still seated on the couch.

She turned around. Tears gleamed in her eyes as she looked at him, sitting, waiting.

"I can't do this. I want to, but I don't think I can." Lexie's voice cracked and the tears began to roll down her cheeks.

Grayson rose from the couch and walked to her, taking her hands in his. "We have to do this. I love you, Lexie, and I don't want to lose you because you're afraid of the 'what if's.'"

He loved her. Her heart swelled as his words sank in. Was she going to lose him because he wore a badge? Was he right and she was a coward? The tears streaming down her cheeks became a flood; her future stood in front her and she only had to reach out for it.

"I didn't think my telling you I loved you would result in tears."

Wiping her eyes, she reached her arms around his neck and kissed him. She pulled back, looking into his face. "I'm sorry I'm crying. I love you too, Grayson. I'm just so damn scared of feeling this way."

He caressed her face. "I'm scared too. But I'm willing if you are." Bending down, he rested his forehead against hers. "I'm sorry about what happened to you. I'm sorry for your loss, but I'm not Kyle. Please remember that."

She jerked back. "How□?"

"It doesn't matter how. I wish I would have heard it from you, but I'm trying to understand why you may have been hesitant to tell me."

She felt weak, like a balloon deflating. She flopped on the couch and bent her head down. "It always seemed so silly when I said it out loud. You are a police officer, something you should be incredibly proud of. How do I tell you that because of Kyle, and your badge, I feel the need to run?"

"Just like that." He sat down beside her and lifted her chin. "You don't have to keep anything from me. Even if you think the words sound silly. I don't think they sound that way at all."

The comfort he offered seeped through her and she leaned into him, lifting her chin, inviting him to kiss her. He caressed the side of her face and slowly traced his thumb across her lips, never taking his eyes from hers. Her blood began to boil and her need for him became unbearable. He pressed his lips to hers and parting them, kissed her deeply, as she indulged in the taste of him, pressing herself closer.

He sat back breathlessly, his eyes filled with questions. Without a word, Lexie stood up, reached for his hand and led him to the bedroom.

Stopping when she reached the bed, she motioned for him to sit. Standing in front of him, she unbuttoned her shirt, letting it fall to the ground. Reaching for her hand, he pulled her closer to him. Wrapping his arms around her waist he leaned in and placed a path of velvet kisses along her naked stomach. His warm breath sent shivers through her body, causing her knees to weaken. Allowing her head to fall back, she arched closer to him, her body demanding more.

Backing away, she held her hands out, and pulled him to stand before her. "I need to feel your skin against mine." Reaching over, she gently slid his sweat pants over his hips. She inhaled sharply, her eyes taking in every inch of the beautiful man before her.

Without taking her eyes from his, she released the clasp on her bra and stepped out of her remaining clothes.

"My God, you're beautiful," Grayson said, pulling her against him.

Laying her gently upon the bed, his hands explored every inch of her, sending spasms throughout her body. Unable to maintain her desire she began an exploration of her own, running her fingers over every defining crevice of his body.

Moaning with pleasure, he lifted himself above her. His eyes radiated with all the love she felt flowing between them. Without taking his eyes from hers, their bodies became one. All recollection of time evaporated until, breathlessly, they fell asleep in each other's arms.

Chapter 15

Waking before the sun, Lexie smiled as she felt Grayson spooned up against her. She ran her fingers along the top of his arm wrapped around her waist. With a wistful sigh, she climbed out of the warm bed, careful not to jostle his arm and wake him.

She grabbed her clothes from the floor and slipped quietly into the bathroom to dress. Tiptoeing across the carpet, she paused to watch him. His dark hair fell over his eye. His face was all angles and lines, like a carved Greek statue, and in strong contrast, he had a small spray of freckles across the bridge of his nose. Her eyes roamed down his jaw line covered in short dark whiskers, and focused on his mouth. She wanted desperately to climb back in beside him and feel those lips on her again.

Instead, she stepped out into the living room and closed the bedroom door behind her. She did have a shop to open after all, and she needed to get home to Ryan so Jordan could get to work. She walked to his desk and opened the drawer looking for a pen and a sheet of paper to leave him a note. Locating a pen, she opened another drawer in search of paper. She rummaged through, and paused when her hand made contact with a picture frame.

Curiosity had her pulling it out and she held it closer to the small desk lamp she'd turned on. She gasped. Grayson stood with his arms around a beautiful brunette in a soft pink tutu and stage make-up. Their eyes were bright and their smiles wide. Their love for each other leapt out of the photograph.

She dropped the framed picture onto the desk as the room began to spin. She braced herself against the edge of the desk, afraid she would pass out. It couldn't be. It wasn't possible.

Tears ran down her cheeks as she picked the photograph up and looked one more time. There was no question: it was Maggie. She turned the picture over and read "New York 2005." Nothing made sense. Who in the hell was Grayson Hunter, really? Tucking it back in the drawer, she raced from the apartment; all thoughts of leaving him a note forgotten.

Still dazed, she'd managed to have her associate open the shop, drop Ryan off at his grandmother's, and fool her brother into thinking her pale complexion was due to lack of sleep.

Sitting outside of Marissa's house her head swirled with unanswered questions and disbelief. She struggled to remember the conversation she'd had with Maggie about her past.

Maggie had just started working for her, and Lexie had called a girl's night at her place. They were sitting together, drinking wine, and grilling Maggie for information.

Maggie laughed. "Well, let's see…I'm originally from Florida, I moved to New York after my parents died to pursue a career in dance. The stages of Broadway were just calling out to me. I worked a bit off Broadway for a while and then followed my heart, which was being carried around by a man, to Washington about three years ago. I lived in the Seattle area for a while, and then wanted a slower pace to raise Ryan, so here I am."

"Dish the dirt on the guy who carried your heart around," Lexie said, leaning forward, curiosity written all over her face. "Spill it, girl."

Maggie's face changed, her smile faded, her eyes grew sad. "There isn't much to tell. He was in the Marines. I met him when he was on leave. Within two weeks, I was a goner and followed him back to the base he was stationed at in Washington. He was shipped off to Iraq, and didn't make it home."

"Oh Maggie, I'm so sorry," Lexie said. "Is he Ryan's father?"

"He was," Maggie answered.

Lexie shook her head before briefly resting it against the steering wheel. She filled her lungs and exhaled slowly, trying to get her emotions under control. Throwing her purse over her shoulder she walked to Marissa's door and knocked.

"Lexie, is everything all right?" Marissa could obviously tell it wasn't. "Come in, I'll pour you some coffee."

She walked into the familiar, bright, open kitchen and sat at the breakfast bar in silence. Marissa set a cup of coffee in front of her and climbed onto the stool beside her.

"Talk to me, what's going on?" Marissa laid her hand over Lexie's.

"I don't think Grayson is dead."

Marissa's eyes drew together. "Why would you have thought he was dead?"

Lexie knew she wasn't making any sense. "I found a picture… of Grayson, in New York. I don't think he's dead."

Marissa shook her head. "Lexie, back up and start at the beginning. I'm not following you."

Lexie took a sip of coffee and a deep breath. "Do you remember Maggie's story about Ryan's father, and how he died in Iraq?"

Nodding, Marissa waited for her to continue.

"I found a picture of Grayson, in New York in 2005. I don't think he's dead."

"What would Grayson's being in New York in 2005 have anything to do with somebody being dead?" Marissa asked.

"It was a picture of him with Maggie."

"Why would Grayson have a picture with…?" Marissa's eyes grew large and her mouth dropped open. "You mean that Grayson is Maggie's dead boyfriend? Why would Maggie tell us he was dead if he wasn't? That doesn't sound like her."

"I don't know." Lexie felt the tears begin again.

Marissa drew in a sharp breath. "Lexie, that would mean—"

"Grayson would also be Ryan's father."

Chapter 16

Later that afternoon, Lexie and Marissa sat side by side on Lexie's couch and stared at the box sitting on the coffee table.

"Lexie, are you sure you're ready to do this?" Marissa asked, lifting the lid of the cardboard box.

"No, I'm not." Lexie took a large swallow from her wine glass. "But I need to."

"You don't really believe that Grayson faked his own death? You know him; do you think he'd be capable of such a thing?"

"No…I don't know. Marissa, what is happening here?" Lexie's hands shook as she set her glass onto the table.

"There has to be another explanation, but none of this makes any sense. He said he loved the girl who left him; she says she loved the man that died in the war. But now, that man may not be dead, she's not here to talk to, and you're not only in love with him, you could possibly be raising his child? Lex, this is crazy." Marissa picked up her own glass and sipped before handing Lexie the tissues.

She'd wanted Marissa here, she'd wanted her support, to lean on her if her world came crashing down, but now she wanted to be alone. She wanted to be able to scream, and yell if she needed to, to throw things, or just curl into a ball and cry if she felt like it. She wanted to curse the fates, before adjusting to the reality that she'd grow old alone.

She'd always believed you only had one chance at real love, and she'd adapted to her fate after Kyle died. Then Grayson showed up and she'd started to believe she'd been gifted with a second chance. Was Grayson so cruel he'd allow Maggie to believe he'd actually died? Did he know about Ryan? Was he using her to be with his son? Was she completely wrong on the timing of it all, and he wasn't ever with Maggie? It was simply an innocent snapshot of two strangers at a Broadway show? But an innocent picture would not be in a frame, tucked inside of a drawer.

Standing up, Lexie began to pace. "I can't do this."

"Are you scared of what you'll find?" Marissa asked, standing up as well.

Lexie whipped around, her eyes full of tears, her heart lodged in her throat. "Hell, yeah, I'm afraid."

Marissa reached over and pulled her into her arms. "I've known you long enough to know you can't bury your head in the sand. You have to know."

Lexie looked up into her best friend's face, and smiled wistfully. "I do."

Lexie opened the lid, and with shaking hands lifted the first item off the top. Nestled inside of a plastic bag for protection was a blue crocheted baby blanket. Setting the bag on the table, she noticed a note inside:

Hand knitted for you with love, Mommy.

Lexie ran her hand over the note, remembering the first time she'd met Maggie, sitting outside of her coffee shop, tears streaming down her face. Maggie's babysitter hadn't shown up and she'd been forced to bring Ryan to her job interview. She'd been so sure his presence would cost her a much needed job that she'd stood outside, crying and apologizing repeatedly for her unprofessional behavior. Lexie had known instantly that they'd be friends as she'd taken Ryan, wrapped in this same blue blanket, into her arms and walked them both into her office and hired Maggie on the spot. At the time, she hadn't known Maggie was dying.

With tears falling unchecked down her face, she reached into the box and pulled out a photo album. She sat back onto the couch, and crossed her legs, balancing the book on her lap. She'd almost forgotten Marissa was there until she slid back beside her, in silent support. She flipped through pictures of Ryan at the hospital, Maggie smiling wide as she bent her head toward her new son, Maggie kissing Ryan's tiny feet, another of her kissing his forehead where the striped knit cap left his baby skin exposed.

With hitching little breaths, she fought for control again. Setting the photo album to the side, she dipped back into the box. Beneath a framed photograph of the new mother looking tenderly upon her new son lay two journals. Lexie lifted them out and set them onto the table before placing the other items gently back into the box and closing the lid.

She walked out onto the patio, and leaning against the railing, pulled the fresh saltwater scented air into her lungs and blew it out slowly. Was she wrong to read these books meant for Ryan? Part of her believed she had no right, but another part of her knew she also had no choice. Looking at the pictures of the two of them, she knew it was no longer just her needing to know for her own selfish reasons. Now she needed to know for both Maggie and for Ryan.

If Grayson was a man capable of lying and leaving Maggie alone to care for a new baby while fighting for her life in a cancer clinic, she needed to know. She would protect Ryan first, and always. She'd made a promise.

Marissa walked onto the patio and without a word, sat down in one of the empty deck chairs and sipped from her wine glass. Lexie picked up the glass Marissa had brought for her and sat back in the other chair overlooking the ocean.

Lexie broke the silence. "Do you remember the day I adopted Ryan?"

"I do."

"Maggie was such a fighter, but that was the day I realized she was losing."

Marissa nodded her head. "Emily Sinclair was with her that day, too. She told us it was happening faster than we expected. Somehow just having her there was comforting; not only for Maggie, but for you as well." Marissa reached over and rested her hand over Lexie's. "Do you remember what you said to Maggie when she woke up that day?"

Lexie had walked over to the bed and felt her chest constrict at the sound of Maggie's labored breathing as tiny wisps of air struggled to escape through her parted, chapped lips. Her body resembled a skeleton beneath the sheet, and her arms lay at her sides, black and blue from the needles keeping her alive. When Maggie had spotted her, her eyes had grown bright.

"I told her, this is where I'm supposed to tell you that you look great, but I'm a terrible liar. You look like hell."

Marissa chuckled. "I couldn't believe you'd said that, but Maggie giggled even though she was trying to look insulted."

"The look on Emily's face was priceless."

"Then it grew serious. It was like everyone knew this was the day."

Lexie wiped the tear from her cheek. "Maggie told me it was her time and that it was worth dying to know she was responsible for bringing Ryan into the world, and to hold him in her arms if only for a short time."

Marissa wiped her eyes on her sleeve. "She was so brave. Ryan was all she cared about. She told you she knew you were the best choice to raise him, and for you to not be afraid because you'd be great." Marissa looked over. "She was right, you know. You're a great mother."

"I promised I would love him enough for both of us."

Marissa nodded her head.

"Then she asked me to make sure Ryan knew how much love she had for him, and to tell him his father would have loved him. To tell Ryan that his father was a hero and she expected nothing less from him."

"You don't know that's not true, Lexie. If Grayson is Ryan's father, there could be another explanation."

Lexie grunted.

"Just keep an open mind."

They sat in silence for a moment, each of them reliving Maggie's final day.

"Then Emily handed me the adoption papers, and Ryan became my world."

"Did I mention you're a great mom?" Marissa added.

"Thank you, but nobody can compare to Maggie. She literally died for her son. How many people would choose to deliver a child at the cost of their own life?"

"I would," Marissa answered. "And so would you."

"She looked so peaceful after the paperwork was signed. It almost made me believe she was okay to leave. I still remember the way her eyes drifted closed as she held tightly to Ryan."

Marissa wiped at the tears on her cheeks again. "But she was able to leave with her baby in her arms and his scent in her final breath."

Unable to speak through her tears, Lexie only nodded.

Chapter 17

Grayson paced. He walked the same path in his living room Lexie had walked the night before. He was worried. He was confused. Last night had been amazing, and tonight, she'd all but vanished. This morning, he'd waken alone; only her spicy, sweet scent lingered as evidence that he hadn't been dreaming. He'd gone to the shop for his morning coffee only to be informed that Lexie wouldn't be in to work that day. She hadn't answered her phone all day, and she hadn't answered her door the three times he'd gone by. He wondered if she was trying to slowly drive him insane. If so, it was working.

Jumping over the couch, he dove for the ringing phone. "Lexie?" He asked breathlessly.

"Well, hello to you too, dear," his mother sneered.

"Hello, Mother." Grayson inhaled and prepared himself for the lecture he knew was lingering on the tip of her tongue.

"And who, may I ask, is Lexie?"

Closing his eyes, he leaned back on the couch and rubbed his temple with his free hand. He wasn't in the mood to get into it with his mother tonight. He needed to talk to Lexie, to know she was okay. He needed to get off the phone and call her again. "I'm sorry I haven't called Mother. I've been meaning to, but I'm on my way out the door. Can I call you tomorrow?"

"Grayson, I haven't heard from you in weeks, and now I hear from someone else, that you were actually shot. Do you have any idea how humiliated I was when I was completely blindsided by this information?" He could hear the familiar disappointment in her tone. "I told you this could happen, but you insisted on becoming a policeman. All those years of education, just wasted, and now—"

"I'm fine, Mother. I had on a vest. I didn't tell you because I didn't want you to worry," Grayson interrupted, hoping to deter her tirade. "I'll tell you all about it, just not tonight. I really have to go."

"You can't spare five minutes for your own mother?" He knew she was working herself into tears. If there was one thing his mother excelled at, it was guilt.

"Can it wait?" He knew he sounded rude, but he'd used up the last of his patience trying to reach Lexie. "I promise I will call you tomorrow."

"No, Grayson, it cannot wait," she snapped. "Your father and I will not be able to attend the Sinclair wedding. Mama's Gold qualified for the Kentucky Derby. Your father and I will be escorting her. Darla will be flying in and attending the wedding with you."

Grayson groaned. Darla Mae Pruitt moved in with his family when she was sixteen years old after her parents died in a car accident. Within six months of that day, his mother was convinced she was destined to be his wife. The truth was he tolerated her because he'd been raised to be proper. She was pretentious, shallow, and entitled, but also convinced with time he would change his mind and they would end up together. Not if she were the last woman on earth.

"Mother, I'm the best man. I can't escort her to the wedding. I have responsibilities to Mark. You know that." He was beginning to panic. The thought of spending a full day with Darla was more than he could bear. "Emily will understand if Darla needs to attend the Derby as well."

"Grayson, Darla is flying in on Friday. I expect you to pick her up and get her settled into her hotel. I also expect you to escort her to the wedding. It's the right thing to do. Darla is not just some girl, and I refuse to have her attending the wedding alone like some desperate simpleton, praying to catch the bouquet."

Grayson stood up and walked to the kitchen. He placed a glass onto the counter and poured a substantial serving of whiskey.

"Mother, I have a date to the wedding. You can't possibly be asking me to escort two women." He hadn't exactly asked Lexie to go with him, but there was no one else he could imagine taking.

"No," his mother spoke slow, punching each word. "I expect you to escort the *right* woman." He could picture his mother's chin shooting into the air, her perfectly made up lips pressed into a thin line. "I expect you to walk into that wedding with Darla on your arm."

"Fine," Grayson said, resigned to his fate, but angry at himself for not refusing his mother's ridiculous demand. "I'll take her, but it will not be a date."

Writing down Darla's flight information, he was finally able to get his mother off the line. Pressing redial, he listened as Lexie's phone once again went unanswered, her recorded voice asking him to leave a message.

Chapter 18

Lexie walked back into the living room and unplugged the phone from the wall. She knew it was Grayson on the other end. Until she knew the truth, he'd have to wait. It wasn't like she could explain anything at this point anyway.

Picking up the journal, she carried it into the bedroom. Crawling under the covers, she opened the book and turned to the first handwritten page.

> *February 2*
> *I can't believe it. I'm pregnant. I'm not sure how I feel right now. I'm excited and scared, petrified really. I'm going to be your mother. Will I be good at this? Will you know how much you mean to me if I have to leave you earlier than I'd want to? Are you a boy with your father's green eyes and a love for motorcycles? Or are you a little girl with dark hair that might love to dance like me? Either way, I can't wait to meet you.*

Lexie took a deep breath, trying to imagine how Maggie felt as she processed the fact that she was going to be a mother. Although she'd never experienced it, she remembered the way she felt when she and Kyle would sit by the ocean and plan the family they'd have together someday. When Kyle died, she'd stopped dreaming of that moment, no longer believing it would ever happen to her. Until the day Maggie placed Ryan in her arms.

Scanning through the next few entries, she froze and returned to the beginning of the entry that brought tears to her eyes.

> *February 17*
> *I've just returned home from Dr. Thorne's office. She wants me to terminate my pregnancy. Well, not necessarily*

wants me to, but insists I must. She doesn't understand that I can't, no matter the consequences to myself. You're already my whole world and you're only the size of a pea. I hoped I would come through this and you would never have to know, but in case that doesn't happen, I should tell you I'm sick. I have the dreaded C word—cancer. After you arrive safely, I promise to fight it with everything I have to ensure our life together is as long as possible. But for now, you come first.

I wish I could talk to your father right now. I know I can't. I ended things with him believing I was doing the right thing. I couldn't take the chance of him worrying about me and putting himself in danger while he's off fighting this terrible war. I'm not condoning lying if it can be avoided, but sometimes it's what you have to do when you truly love someone. You put yourself last, caring more for the other person than your wants or needs. You'll be like that. You won't have any other choice; it's in your genes already. Your father is going to love you so much. He's wanted you forever. He'll be an amazing father. He has so much love to give. I hope you'll understand someday why I must still keep my illness a secret from him, but he needs to know about you. He deserves to know. You deserve to know him.

Setting the journal down on the bed, Lexie walked into the bathroom and splashed water on her tear stained face. Maggie had loved Ryan so much. Lexie understood even more that being asked to raise Ryan was an honor, a sacred trust, and a blessing. Maggie had given Lexie the most important, precious piece of herself, and she was going to make sure that Maggie was proud of the way she raised Ryan.

Visions of Grayson's green eyes danced through her mind as she again wondered if he was Ryan's father. Nothing made sense.

She had to know the truth. Climbing back under the covers, she continued to read, skimming through the details of Maggie's doctor appointments, and endless tiredness. She stopped again and carefully re-read an entry.

May 2

I can't believe this has happened. The pain is like nothing I've experienced before. I can't breathe, I can't think, I don't want to get out of bed. I can tell you're sensing my sadness, as you are tossing and turning inside of me, unable to rest. I can't believe I have to tell you this. I can't seem to get the words to come off my pen and onto the paper. My sweet baby, your father died.

I called his family to find him so I could tell him about you. Instead, I'm left with this hole in my heart in knowing you will never have the joy of knowing him. Please remember he was a hero. The strongest man I've ever known, filled with duty, and the passion to always fight for what he believed was right.

I've been spending a lot of time trying to find the perfect name for you, and today I know. If you are a girl, I'm going to call you Hunter Anne, after your father and your grandmother, if you're a boy, Ryan Hunter, after your grandfather and your father. I'm so sorry that you won't ever meet him, or that he will never meet you. I promise you one thing though; I will love you enough for all of us.

Tears stung Lexie's eyes as the proof began to gather. She closed the journal, unable to read further through the panic rising inside her. Could this still be a crazy coincidence? She didn't think so.

Lexie knew that Maggie's parents had passed years ago, but if Maggie had contacted the father's parents wouldn't she have told them she was pregnant with his child? Wouldn't they have wanted to know Ryan, to be a part of his life? If that was so, why did Maggie tell her that there was no one else to care for Ryan? And where were they now? So many things didn't make sense. The main questions remained unanswered. If Grayson was the father, why did Maggie believe he was dead? And did Grayson know he had a son?

Lexie knew with every question answered, hundreds more would arise. Her mind was swirling, like a tornado across the ocean, picking up speed, and gathering more questions with each turn. Opening the journal again, she continued to read.

> *May 14*
> *Our lease is almost up, and there isn't any reason for us to stay here. I think you and I need a fresh start. I'm getting too big to teach dance at the studio for much longer and I want you and I settled in before you make your grand entrance. With the world at our fingertips, it wasn't an easy decision to pick one place to plant our roots, but I've decided on California. It's certainly a change from Washington, with its continuous rain, but I'm tired of being cold. There, we can play in the waves at the beach, and drive into San Francisco to walk on the wharf. I think this could be an amazing adventure for us. There is also a wonderful treatment facility there. My doctor tells me there is a much better chance they can help me than most other places. Sounds like the perfect choice, don't you think? I know you can't know this, but as I'm rubbing my stomach, you're kicking me back. I'm taking this as a yes from you. Next weekend, we are packing up and driving out to start our first big adventure together.*

Closing the journal, Lexie set it on the table and walked into her bedroom. She slipped on her pajamas and reached for her robe. Tears flooded her eyes when one of Grayson's t-shirts slipped from the hook and fell to the floor. Picking it up, she lifted it to her nose, breathing in the familiar scent of him. Her heart lurched, the ache becoming unbearable. She had to know. Dropping the shirt back to the floor, she rushed from the room and picked up the journal again in search of answers.

Chapter 19

It had been thirty-two hours and twenty-two minutes since he'd fallen asleep with Lexie in his arms. Thirty-two hours, twenty-two minutes, and forty-two seconds since he'd heard the sound of her voice. It was like he no longer fully existed without her. He'd thought he'd been in love before, but this was different, more. He wanted to hold her in his arms every night for the rest of his life. He wanted to read Dr. Seuss to Ryan and drive him to little league practice. He wanted it all. And he wanted it with Lexie.

After the pain he'd endured in his last relationship, he'd sworn he'd never fall in love again. To be honest, he'd never thought he was capable of feeling for anyone else. Then he'd met Lexie. One look in her amber eyes and something had shifted inside him.

He believed there was only one person in the world, a soul mate you could say, for everyone; he'd thought he'd lost his. Without any explanation, the woman he'd believed to be that person for him had walked away. The pain had seemed unbearable at times as he'd lie on his cot desperately trying to understand what had gone wrong. She'd never called the number he'd sent in his letters, never gave him the courtesy to explain. There were times he'd wondered if she'd moved, or maybe she didn't want to send him a "Dear John" letter. He'd only been able to get a call out to her twice. Once he'd gotten her machine and begged her to change her mind, the second time he'd gotten a disconnected notice. It was clear. She'd walked away from him, and the life they'd planned together.

Sitting down on the couch, he quickly rose again, and began to pace the room. He felt wound as tight as a spring, but as out of control as a slinky down a set of stairs. Lexie had to talk to him. He refused to let her run away from him. He still believed in the soul mate scenario, but he'd learned that someone could be wrong in recognizing them. Or maybe he was wrong that there was only one. Lexie was meant to be with him. He'd known that almost immediately. Now he had to somehow convince her. If he'd been unable to get her off his mind then, it was impossible to do so now.

So why wouldn't she talk to him? He had replayed the night over and over again in his mind, and each time was more confused than the time before. He was worried, and scared that he'd somehow lost her. He *had* to talk to her. Grabbing his helmet, he rushed from the room.

The wind blew warm across his body as he rounded the turn and accelerated his motorcycle down the highway along the shore. What was he going to do if she didn't open the door? Maybe he'd call in the SWAT team with their battering ram and knock her door down. Maybe he would just curl up on her front step and wait for her to come out. She'd have to leave sometime.

Pulling up beside her car, he parked his bike, removed his helmet and marched up the stairs. His breathing was shallow, his stomach queasy, and his heart pounded in his ears. He wiped his sweaty palms on the front of his jeans and knocked on her door.

He stepped back and waited. When she didn't answer, he placed his ear to the door, listening for any noise from inside. Hearing nothing, he wondered if she could be asleep, it was after eleven. But then again, he didn't care. If he had to wake her up and make her talk to him, he would. Raising his fist he knocked again, this time more of a pounding than a knock.

"Lexie, open the door!" he shouted.

When the door remained closed, he pounded again. Minutes later, he sighed and turned to leave, wondering if his worst fear was going to happen again.

*

The pounding at the door finally stopped as Lexie sat quietly in the dimly lit room. Pulling her feet onto the couch and her knee's to her chest, she rested her forehead against them and let the tears flow.

Hesitant to read on, she'd put the journal down. Now it was staring back at her. Mocking her, daring her to finish what she'd started. The truth was she was scared to know. If Grayson was the father, what did that mean? Had he been so angry with Maggie leaving that he'd let her believe he was dead? Did he know she was sick and still turn his back on her? Could he have known she was carrying his child and choose to be absent from Ryan's life? It didn't seem like something he could do, but maybe she wasn't seeing him clearly. Did she love him so much she'd become a blind fool?

There were very few circumstances she could conjure up that would make any of this forgivable. She reached up and rubbed her chest, as if slow clockwise circles could somehow ease the pain. She took a sip of water, trying to force the cool liquid past the tennis-ball-sized lump in her throat. Setting the glass back onto the table, she lifted the journal and opened it where she'd left off. Scanning through the pages, she skimmed over packing, hot dog cravings, the inability to sleep for more than two hours at a time, and the description of their new apartment. Gasping, Lexie reached over and turned the lamp up one click brighter and returned to the top of the page.

June 1

We're finally here sweetheart. I can't wait to show you our new home. We can't see the ocean from our new apartment but we can smell it, and it's only a short stroll to the beach. Being here brings up so many memories of my time with your father. We'd always talked about moving here and raising the family we'd have one day. How I wish he were here with us now. I wish he could see that the future we'd dreamt of was happening. That he would be here to greet you when you finally make your appearance, to hold you in his strong arms. I want to watch his face soften as he looks into your eyes, and see him pull you closer and keep you safe. I have a confession to make to you. I've done omething I will regret forever, and that I need to apologize to you for. Selfishly, before I knew of you, I threw away the pictures of your father and me. At the time it was just too painful, and I knew I needed to make a complete break from him to keep him safe. Now, I know I've destroyed the only ties you had to him. Grayson Hunter was an amazing...

Lexie's lungs burst out the breath she didn't realize she was holding. Her body began to shake, and the pain that had settled in her chest erupted and flowed through her entire body. The journal dropped to the floor as she curled up into the fetal position and sobbed.

Chapter 20

Aimee Morrison stood beside the open door of the limousine, her hand resting on her jutted hip and scowled at Lexie.

"It's my bachelorette party and my bridesmaid can't bail on me. You're going, you have to."

Even as she tried to look disappointed, Aimee glowed. Lexie couldn't remember seeing anyone as in love as Aimee was with Mark. The sunlight reflected off the diamond engagement ring, handed down from her mother, causing small patches of light to sparkle across the black limousine. She wore a silky red dress that left one shoulder bare, incredibly high heels, with an Amoré silver bag hanging from her shoulder. She looked sexy and sophisticated at the same time.

Lexie tilted her head and sighed in defeat. She knew she was being selfish, but hadn't been able to snap out of her sadness. With her life unraveling, she was struggling to muster the strength to smile and laugh with her friends.

Marissa stuck her head out of the door, "Come on, Lexie, a couple of shots and some loud music and you'll be fine." She drew back into the limo and patted the seat beside her. "Let's get this party started."

Sliding in beside Marissa, she made room for the bride-to-be. Glasses of champagne were already being passed around, and Luther, the man of honor, was attempting to find the right music on the sound system.

As the limousine pulled out of the gates of the Sinclair Estate, Lexie tossed back her glass of champagne, and held it out for Luther to refill. She pushed her thoughts of Grayson, Maggie, and Ryan to the back of her mind. Tonight was about Aimee. The rest of the world would still be there in the morning.

Marissa leaned over and whispered in her ear, "Welcome back, I've missed you."

Lexie leaned her head on Marissa's shoulder for a moment. She knew Marissa had been worried about her, but she hadn't pushed, or judged. She'd silently stood by and waited for the time Lexie was ready to take her next step.

"Turn it up, Luther!" Aimee yelled excitedly, and the entire group sang along to the song now blaring through the speakers.

By the time they arrived at their destination, Lexie was comfortably numb on multiple glasses of champagne. An extremely large bald man in a navy blue suit lifted the end of the red rope blocking the entrance, and stood back for them to enter. "Welcome back, Miss Aimee," he smiled and bowed his head in greeting. "Nice to see you again, Miss Lexie," his eyes scanned from the top of her head to the tips of red painted toes. "You look beautiful tonight."

"Thank you, Frank. You're looking large, strong and handsome tonight yourself."

Taking a step, Lexie swayed, and bumped sideways into Luther. Taking her arm, Luther held her upright and led her into the dimly lit lounge. "I'm not sure I've ever seen you tipsy, Lexie."

"I'm not tipsy," Lexie insisted. "I'm just not used to wearing heels."

Luther chuckled, but said nothing as he helped her onto the stool beside Aimee. The waitress arrived with three more bottles of champagne in a large ice bucket, and began to pour each of them a flute.

"Tequila, we all need shots of tequila," Lexie stated.

"I don't think that's such a good idea," Marissa shook her head, her pleading eyes circling the table in search of back up.

"We're here to have a good time. Our Aimee is getting married in a few days. It's our last big girl's night before she's an old married woman like you, Marissa." Lexie laughed at her own joke, waving unsteadily on her stool.

"Tequila," Luther seconded, and raised his champagne glass

in the air. "To girl's night!" The group laughed at Luther. He appeared to have no issues being the only man at a bachelorette party. "When's the stripper getting here?"

"Luther, behave yourself," Aimee scolded. "There will be no strippers. I'm not having you run off with some man in a thong three days before my wedding. It's for your own good."

Luther sighed and passed around the shots of tequila, raised his shot glass in the air inviting everyone to toast. Lexie slammed her empty glass onto the table, and greedily sucked on a lime wedge.

The band was setting up, the sounds of guitar strings plucking, microphones tapping, and directions being shouted out to the men setting the lights filled the room. Another group of Aimee's girlfriends entered the private lounge, bringing with them another round of tequila.

The music played, champagne flowed, and high heels began to pile up on the side of the busy dance floor. Lexie swayed to the music, singing at the top of her lungs. She knew she was going to pay for her alcohol consumption in the morning, but tonight, she felt better than she had in days. Walking over to the bar, she ordered another round.

Marissa walked up beside her. "Lexie, don't you think you've had enough?"

"Nope," Lexie slurred. "Just about right, I think." She pushed a shot glass into Marissa's hand and clanked hers against it before emptying it. She reached over and lifted the still full glass from Marissa's hand and emptied that as well. "Come dance," she shouted, pulling Marissa behind her onto the dance floor.

When the band stopped to take a break, Lexie made her way into the restroom. She braced herself against the walls of the stall, trying to keep the world from spinning. She didn't want to get sick. Marissa wouldn't let her hear the end of it.

She heard the door open and the sound of rubber heels squeaking against the stone tiled floor.

"You know she's a total fraud," one of the female voices said. "Got to give her credit though, she did a much better job convincing Emily Sinclair she was her long-lost daughter than I did. I never thought to get Mark into bed."

"Molly, you're terrible. Why would you offer to work tonight? You knew who the private party was," asked the other.

"I needed to see her in person. Aimee Morrison is my hero, working Emily over the way she did."

Lexie felt the heat rise on her face. Her hands clenched as the urge to strike grew strong.

"Be careful." She heard the sound of running water. "If Emily Sinclair shows up and sees you, you'll lose your job, hell, you could even go back to jail. Isn't it in your restraining order that you can't go near her?"

"She's not coming, or she'd be here already. She doesn't leave her *palace* often anyway. She's probably rolling around in her money wearing nothing but her diamonds." The girl laughed at her own joke.

Lexie peeked through the crack of the stall door. She could see a brunette straightening her pony tail, and applying lip gloss. Lexie recognized her as one of the waitresses. She couldn't see the other girl's face, but she was blonde, also with her hair pulled up, and wearing a chef's jacket.

When the girl came into view Lexie's mouth dropped open. She couldn't believe it. Standing in the bathroom mirror was Emily Sinclair's old assistant. The con artist who'd claimed to be Emily's kidnapped daughter and embezzled a large amount of money from her. The girl had gone to jail, but she'd broken Emily's heart and for that alone, Lexie hated her. She could feel the hairs stand up on the back of her neck and her blood pounding through her system. How dare she be here?

"I just can't believe that she fell for the lost daughter routine again." The girl chuckled. "I've got to hand it to Aimee Morrison, she's good, real good. I wonder how much money she'll squeeze out of ole' *mommy* before she bolts. I wish I could find a way to crash the wedding. Really see how a pro works."

Lexie yanked open the stall door, heat creeping up her cheeks, fists clenched. She knew it was partly the alcohol in her system making her feel invincible, but Lexie liked the fear she saw in the girl's eyes once she'd recognized her.

Without a word, Lexie lifted her fist and punched the girl in the jaw, causing her to stumble back against the bathroom counter. The brunette stared at her for a moment and bolted from the room. Lexie didn't see it coming but felt the blow to her temple as her legs buckled and she fell against the stall door. She'd never been a fighter, but tonight, the urge to wipe the smirk from the girl's face was too strong to ignore. Could it have been the tequila, or was it as simple as right versus wrong? Either way, tonight she didn't care.

Lexie reached out, and grabbing the front of the girl's jacket, pulled her closer, standing nose to nose with her. "You're scum," Lexie sneered. "How dare you insult Emily after all you've done?"

The girl threw her hands up. "Let me go, I'll leave right now."

Lexie shoved her back against the counter and lifted her arm to strike again. She didn't get the chance. Marissa stood behind her, holding tightly to her arm.

"She's not worth it, Lex," Marissa said calmly.

"Do you know who she is?" Lexie swooned, suddenly feeling dizzy. "She deserves much worse than this."

Wrapping her arm around her, Marissa led Lexie from the bathroom and sat her in an empty chair. "You're a feisty drunk."

"I am not drunk." Lexie stated, before realizing that her words were actually slurred. "Well maybe I am, but she still deserved it. Do you know who that was?"

"I do. The waitress came out and told me what was happening." Marissa filled a napkin with ice and placed it against Lexie's temple. "Does it hurt?"

She reached up and held the napkin against her cut. "No, it doesn't hurt. That's bad, huh?" Lexie leaned her head on Marissa's shoulder. "You mad at me?"

"No, I'm not mad at you, but you're going to be mad at yourself in the morning." Marissa gently rubbed her back. "Jordan is on his way to pick you up."

Lexie shot upright and groaned when the world began to spin. "You didn't tell him I was actually in a fight did you?"

"Of course I did!" Marissa laughed. "I wouldn't have missed hearing his reaction for the world, and I'm excited to hear the lecture he's come up with during the drive."

Lexie snarled and laid her head onto the table awaiting her brother's wrath.

Chapter 21

Grayson took a deep breath. This was not going to go well. He was sure of that. When Jordan called and asked him to rescue Lexie from the bachelorette party, he hadn't hesitated. He also didn't consider the fact that Lexie hadn't spoken to him in over a week, or that she was clearly intoxicated, or even the fact that he had someone in the car.

"Stay here," he told Darla Mae. "I'll be right back."

"But I want to say hello to Aimee," she pouted. "I don't want to wait in the car."

"Stay here. I mean it." He'd picked her up from the airport less than an hour ago and was already fed up with her.

Heading for the entrance, he was suddenly blocked by a large man with a bald head and a don't-mess-with-me growl. "We're closed tonight; private party."

"I realize that," Grayson continued, taking a step back so he could look into the man's face. "I'm here to pick up one of the guests. It seems she's had too many glasses of champagne."

"The guest's name?" His eyes drew together, and his voice was deep and gravelly, not to mention a bit intimidating.

"Lexie Wayne."

Grayson hadn't thought it possible, but the man stood even taller, pushing his chest out. "And who are you?"

From the looks of it, this man had a crush on his girl. Was Lexie still his girl? At this point, he wasn't sure.

Deciding it best to leave out the details of their relationship he replied, "I'm a friend, and her brother's partner. He asked me to pick her up because I was already in town."

The bouncer looked over his head and seemed to relax when he spotted Darla Mae sitting in the car. "Lexie is a spunky one," he said. "She let some girl have it in the restroom." His laugh sounded like a high-powered chain saw. "I wouldn't want to be on the receiving end of her wrath." He looked Grayson up and down again, before stepping to the side. "Go on in, and let me know if you need any help getting her to the car."

Nodding his head, Grayson strode into the dimly lit room and followed the noise into another section of the club. He watched as the women danced in a circle around Aimee's best friend Luther. Most of the women were barefoot, some had drinks in hand, and by the looks of it, the majority of them were passing tipsy and headed straight for drunk.

Not seeing Lexie, he wandered closer to the bar itself. His heart pounded when he spotted her sitting beside Marissa, her head down against the table. He knew he'd missed her, but until he saw her, even he didn't realize how much.

He recognized the moment Marissa spotted him. Her expressive face portrayed a combination of relief and worry. He wished he had time to find out if Marissa would confide in him what was going on with Lexie, but he knew he didn't. Darla Mae wouldn't sit waiting in the car much longer, and it was already going to be an interesting ride home once Lexie met her.

"Hello Grayson," Marissa greeted, a smile pasted on her face. "I thought Jordan was coming to pick up Lexie?"

"He was, but I was already in town and offered to save him the drive." Watching Marissa's face, he knew that whatever happened with Lexie was worse than he thought. He wished he had at least a small clue of what he'd done wrong.

She looked over at Lexie and then quickly back to him as if she were somehow reluctant to let her friend go with him. Grayson put his hand on Marissa's shoulder and waited for her to look up at him. "I will drive her home. That's it."

"Grayson, what are you doing here?"

They both spun around at the sound of Lexie's voice.

"I'm taking you home. Jordan called me because I was already in town." He hated that he felt the need to immediately explain his presence. Walking over to her, his chest tightened when he met her wary eyes.

"I can't get on your motorcycle in this dress." Lexie snapped. She stood up, swaying from left to right. "I'll be fine. I'll just wait for Aimee and ride back in the limo."

"I didn't bring the bike." Grayson struggled to keep his voice calm. He wanted to scream and yell, demand she tell him what was happening. More than that, he wanted to pull her into his arms, and feel her head against his chest.

Lexie plopped down on the chair and let her head fall back. "I don't feel good."

Grayson looked at Marissa, and without a word, they each took one of her arms and lifted Lexie from the chair. Her knees buckled, and Lexie jerked forward, causing Marissa to lose her grip. Grayson caught her and swung her into his arms like she were a small child.

Exiting the lounge, he nodded to the bouncer and waited for the large man to open the back door of the car. He slid Lexie onto the seat and fastened her seatbelt. Her head was bobbing up and down, her eyes closed and her hands grasped tightly on her lap.

Suddenly, her head shot up. "My shoes, Grayson, I need my shoes." Finally focusing on Darla Mae, Lexie's eyes drew into slits. "Didn't mean to interrupt your date," she sneered.

Grayson paused in the open door, and crouched down. "I'm not on a date, Lexie. You know me better than that."

"Do I? Do I really know you, Grayson Hunter?" Lexie barked.

He snapped back as if she'd slapped him. Her tone was accusing, but her eyes filled with unshed tears. What was going on with her?

"This is Darla Mae Pruitt from Kentucky. She lives with my folks. Remember, I told you about her?" Grayson reached over and laid his hand over Lexie's. "I just picked her up from the airport. She's in town for the wedding."

Looking from Lexie to Darla, he cringed at the look of disgust on Darla's face as she watched Lexie.

Obviously, still drunk and looking for a fight, Lexie glared back at her. "What's your problem?"

Darla Mae's mouth opened in a perfectly formed O, as she sat there incredulous. Grayson cleared his throat in an attempt to cover the snicker that slipped from his lips. He couldn't remember the last time he'd seen Darla Mae speechless.

Trying to regain some control over the situation, Grayson stood and closed the door to the backseat before climbing in behind the wheel. "Marissa is bringing your shoes. We will drop Darla Mae at her hotel, and then I will drive you home."

Grayson looked over his shoulder when the back seat remained silent. Lexie was sound asleep; her head tilted back, her mouth slightly parted. Even drunk, she was the most beautiful woman he'd ever seen.

Darla Mae sighed, "Really, Grayson? That's the type of woman you want?"

"Don't," he spat, turning to her. "I will not have you say one more word, is that understood?"

She crossed her arms and turned to stare out the window, not speaking until they pulled up at her hotel.

"Thank you for the ride," was all she said as she walked through the glass doors.

Lexie was still asleep when they arrived at her condo. He fished her keys out of her purse, and lifted her into his arms again.

Stirring, Lexie looked up at him before laying her head back against his shoulder. "I wish I never met you," she mumbled, her eyes still closed. "I want my heart back."

Grayson felt the sting behind his eyes as the pain sliced through him.

Chapter 22

The day of Aimee's wedding was warm and sunny, with a faint breeze blowing the scent of roses through the air. Lexie, in a scarlet colored silk dress and strappy silver heels, walked through the yard in search of Emily, the mother of the bride, and one of her dearest friends.

White chairs sat facing a large arbor decorated in white lights, tulle, and thousands of white roses. Lexie skirted around a long white runner creating an aisle that ran from the back porch between the chairs and ended at the platform beneath the arbor. Emily was adjusting the flower arrangements that sat on tall white pillars on each side of the platform.

"It looks beautiful," Lexie said, stepping up beside her.

Emily turned to her, tears of joy glimmered in her eyes. "It really does, doesn't it?" She smiled. "My little girl is getting married today," she said more to herself. "I still can't believe it."

"Aimee's asking for you," Lexie told her, taking Emily's arm. "She said she won't put on her dress until you're there to button her."

A single tear rolled down her cheek, her green eyes filled with such happiness, she glowed brighter than the sun. "Well, let's go."

Walking into the large room that had been transformed into the bridal suite, Aimee sat at the vanity while a woman wearing a black smock pulled her blonde curls into a soft pile on her head. Emily walked over and whispered something in her daughter's ear. When Lexie saw the perfect picture of mother and daughter reflected back at her through the mirror, she felt her eyes well up with tears. Looking over, she saw Marissa was wiping her eyes as well.

She could still remember the years before Aimee and Emily found each other, the sense of loss and loneliness that was always a part of Emily. But today, as they looked into each other's eyes, the resemblance was unquestionable, both their appearance and their matching radiance.

Understanding the pain Emily endured not knowing where her daughter was for twenty-eight years, made her wonder again if Grayson knew he had a child. Did he study the face of each child he came across, searching for similarities as Emily had? Had he turned his back on his child, not wishing to have a part in his life? If he somehow didn't know, would she lose her son once he did?

"Lexie, are you all right?"

Lost in her own thoughts, she hadn't seen Aimee slip into her dress. She was stunning. "Yes, I'm so sorry. Aimee, you are the most beautiful bride I've ever seen."

Aimee's cheeks flushed. "Thank you very much. But you haven't seen the best part." Lifting her dress, she stuck her foot out. Her shoes were clear with a slight hint of iridescent shading. "Mark had these made for me. True glass slippers," she gushed.

"You are going to be so very happy," Lexie told her and wrapped her arms around her friend.

Ryan bolted through the door clad in a black tux with a red cummerbund, his face bright and excited. "Mom, look," he said, spinning in a circle. "I look just like Grayson. I even got a flower in my ladle."

"I think you mean your lapel," Lexie chuckled.

The women in the room circled around him, cooing over how handsome he was, calling him dapper, and telling him he would surely outshine the groom himself. Ryan grinned from ear to ear. Looking up, Lexie met Emily's gaze, her eyes questioning, and her concern clear.

Lexie smiled in reassurance, and knelt down to the same level as her son. "You have the rings?" she asked. When he nodded, she asked, "You know what to do?"

Ryan nodded his head with such force, he stumbled back a step. "Don't lose the rings, don't trip, and remember to hold the pillow up so Mark doesn't have to bend down and ruin the pictures." He spoke like reading from an imaginary checklist. "Oh, and don't pick my nose. Grayson told me that one."

As the room erupted with laughter, Lexie felt a sharp pain pierce her heart. If Grayson didn't know Ryan was his son, was her not telling him robbing him of a tremendous memory as he helped Ryan dress in his first tuxedo?

She felt eyes on her and looked up at Emily, worry etched on her face. "Lexie, can I see you in the hall for a moment?"

Marissa bobbed her head, motioning Lexie should go. Unsure of her voice, she nodded her head, smiled faintly and followed Emily into the hall.

"Are you okay?" Emily asked. "What's going on? You look on the verge of tears, and Grayson is walking around like someone has died. Are you two arguing?"

Lexie's smile came easily at the question. It would be so much easier if they were simply arguing, but it was much larger than that. "No, we're not arguing, just trying to work some things out." She answered honestly. "Don't you dare worry about me today. Your daughter is getting married. This is a big day for both of you."

Emily wrapped her arms around Lexie, and when she pulled back, her face was radiant. "I never thought it was possible to be this happy, to live this life. I can't believe my daughter is finally home. How many parents spend their lives mourning the child they lost, or pace the floors every day wondering if they will ever have them back because someone has kept them apart? I'm so blessed; I feel my heart might explode from being over filled."

It was impossible not to feel the joy that exuded from Emily. It was equally impossible not to feel as if her words were speaking directly to her and her situation with Grayson. She knew she had to talk to him. Now wasn't the time, but the least she could do was let him know she was ready to talk. That she needed to.

Besides, every inch of her felt his close proximity. He had become an invisible magnet she was powerless to resist. She wanted to see him, drink him in. To somehow just glance at him and know he wasn't malicious, or vengeful. To know that he would explain everything to her and it would all be all right.

"Go on inside and be with your daughter." Lexie hugged Emily tightly. "You've been more help than you know. I think I'm going to sneak away and find Grayson."

Chapter 23

Holding tightly to Ryan's hand, Grayson headed for the kitchen hoping to find a snack for Ryan who was insistent he'd die at any moment from starvation. As they came through the swinging door, Mimsey, the family cook, looked up from the tray she was arranging.

"You shouldn't be in here; you don't want to get anything on your tuxes." She said, her mouth stern but her eyes smiling.

Grayson laughed. Obviously dressed for the wedding, she wore a glittery gold dress with an apron covering the front. Her hair was pulled on top of her head in a pile of curls, her face, the color of hot chocolate, was lightly covered in make-up, her lips tinted in a dark shade of peach.

"You shouldn't be in here either, Mimsey." Grayson walked over and kissed her cheek. "Emily is going to kill you if she finds you in here working today."

Mimsey blushed and bowed her head for a moment. Straightening her back, her fingers resumed their work on the tray. "She will never know." She looked over at him, her eyes drawing together. "I cannot allow these caterers to mess up my Aimee's wedding day. They are sloppy and careless. It must be perfect, even if I have to do it myself."

The kitchen door swung open and a young girl in a black vest and a bow tie stopped abruptly when she spotted Mimsey. Grayson cleared his throat and bowed his head in attempt to hide the smile on his face. The poor girl looked terrified.

"Don't just stand there," Mimsey snapped. "Bring in those trays. I have done one for you the correct way. I expect you to prep the others in the exact same way. Do you think you can handle that?"

The girl nodded her head and stepped over to study the completed tray in front of Mimsey.

Startled, Grayson looked down when the edge of his jacket was tugged. Ryan looked up at him and whispered, "Is Mimsey gonna let us eat something or will she be mad?"

Reaching his arm around Ryan's shoulders, Grayson winked. "Mimsey, poor Ryan here is starving. We're afraid he could faint during the ceremony if he's not nourished soon."

As he'd predicted, Mimsey came around the counter, a smile stretching from ear to ear on her face. "Mr. Ryan, how handsome you look," she cooed, "How about a sandwich, something that can't drip on your sharp clothes?" She took hold of his hand and led him to the table in the corner of the kitchen.

"Mimsey, can I trust you to bring Ryan back up to the groom's suite after he finishes his lunch? I need to go find Lexie." It was becoming physically painful for him, knowing she was so close and not being with her. He needed to see her, desperately.

"You run along, Grayson, Ryan and I will be just fine," she replied, setting a small glass of milk onto the table in front of him.

Winking at Ryan, he headed out of the kitchen and up the winding stairs. Reaching the top, he sucked in his breath. Lexie stood in the hallway outside the bridal suite talking to Emily. She was stunning in a silky red dress that accentuated the curve of her hips and the swell of her breasts. Her red painted toes peeked out beneath the flow of the fabric embraced by jeweled silver straps. His eyes roamed back upwards taking in every inch of her. Her dark hair was piled loosely on the top of her head, leaving her neck exposed, and small ringlets fell randomly on either side. As she turned to embrace Emily, he saw that her dress was open at the back, pooling softly at her waist, and a long silver chain hung down between her shoulder blades and stopped at her lower back.

After Emily had disappeared through the door, Lexie turned and began walking toward him. He knew the moment she'd spotted him. Frozen in place, she simply stared at him; her eyes flashed a mixture of panic and yearning.

"You look exquisite, Lex," he told her, unsure of what to say to keep her from running away.

Noticing the faint blush on her cheeks, he took one tentative step toward her. Tears glistened in her eyes and her body tensed, but she didn't retreat.

"I needed to see you," he admitted. "I've been so worried."

Simply nodding her head, she swallowed hard, her neck flexing with the effort. "Grayson, we need to talk."

"I would like that," he replied, taking one step closer, his eyes locked on hers.

She opened her mouth to speak, and then snapped it closed again. Taking one final step, he stood in arm's reach before her. Her expressive eyes were a slide show of emotions, but beneath it all, he recognized he hadn't completely lost her. Slowly, he lifted his hand to her cheek and felt a reassuring warmth when she tilted her head against his palm. Tentatively, he tilted her head toward him and lightly brushed his lips over hers. Digging his nails into the palm of his hands to distract himself long enough to gain his self-control, he deepened the kiss, feeling her body melt against his.

Lexie brought her hands to his chest, and halfheartedly attempted to push him away. Breathlessly she mumbled, "I can't do this yet. Not until we talk." She stepped back, but left her hands resting against his chest. "It's important."

Nodding, Grayson tilted her chin back so she was forced to look at him. "Tonight, promise me we'll talk tonight." When she nodded her reply, he bent forward to kiss her gently one more time.

"Grayson, darling," a voice called out, shattering the connection between them. "Where are you?"

Lexie's spine stiffened and her eyes shot daggers aimed directly for his heart. She turned and hurried back down the hallway without a word.

He called after her, but knew his attempt was futile. Damn that Darla Mae Pruitt, he knew she would be trouble.

Chapter 24

The ceremony was beautiful. Aimee seemed to float above the ground as she walked down the aisle on the arm of her "Uncle" Bob, her eyes solely focused on her groom standing beneath the arbor. After Bob had given Aimee's hand to Mark, he sat in the empty seat beside Emily. Lexie was surprised to see him bend over and kiss her softly on the lips. In all the years she'd worked with Emily she'd never known her to have a man in her life. It was heartwarming to realize that she'd gotten her daughter back, and seemed to have discovered a second chance at love.

Lexie walked into the tent-covered reception area and gazed around at the beauty of it all. Tall white chairs circled round tables draped in white cloth. Red and white roses splashed out of the center of each table surrounded by white candles burning in crystal holders. White china with silver etching boasted a pair of wedding bells on each plate, along with the couple's names and the date. More roses cascaded out of tall urns throughout the area and surrounded all four sides of the dance floor set over the grass. The head table sat at one end of the dance floor and was U shaped so the wedding party could visit with each other and still enjoy the other guests.

She made her way to the head table and froze when she realized who she'd been seated next to. She'd made it a point to avoid all eye contact with Grayson during the ceremony, but hadn't considered the fact they'd be seated together at the reception. Of course, why wouldn't they be? Until now they'd been dating, and they were both part of the wedding party. She wanted to run. She wanted to cry. What she didn't want to do was sit beside Grayson and battle her emotions for the next four hours. She didn't think she was strong enough.

Darla Mae Pruitt entered the reception area and walked directly to Grayson's side. She stood regally in her designer dress, sipping from a crystal champagne flute. Lexie felt her blood begin to boil when Darla Mae whispered into Grayson's ear.

Turning away, Lexie made her way through the clusters of people enjoying the sunshine and conversation, crossed the yard, and let herself in the back door of the house. Her hands shook as she opened the door and slipped inside the bridal suite.

The room was empty. The aftermath of the morning all that remained. Garment bags were draped over chairs, hair brushes and bobby pins strewn upon the vanities, and empty champagne glasses were lined up along the fireplace mantel.

Lexie pushed aside an abandoned robe and plopped into the chair, tilting her head against the silky back. Closing her eyes for a moment, she wished she could curl up and sleep the rest of the day away. She didn't want to see Grayson dancing and smiling with another woman. She didn't want to watch how wonderful he was with her son or see Ryan's eyes light up every time Grayson spoke. Her son loved Grayson. Her son. The words echoed in her head. Ryan was no longer simply her son; now, by some bizarre act of fate, he was their son. Why did that thought terrify her and yet send butterflies fluttering in her stomach?

Telling him, actually saying the words aloud, would change everything in all of their lives. She wished she could be certain that Grayson hadn't abandoned Maggie when she needed him most. Or that he hadn't just gone about his life knowing he had a son who needed him. And what if he knew Ryan was his son and he'd used her to get closer to him? That he'd never loved her at all.

The room began to swim around her, her eyes struggled to focus, her breathing shallow. She gulped for air, and leaned her head against her knees in an attempt to stop the spinning. Logically she knew there would be no benefit for Grayson to use her to get to Ryan, but she couldn't help but fear it could be true. Maybe she never knew him at all, and he was going to single handedly destroy her entire life.

Standing up on shaky legs, she peered at her reflection in the mirror. Her color was a bit flushed, but she didn't appear like a woman who only seconds ago was close to fainting. It was time for her to get herself together, and go enjoy her friend's special day. She'd smile as Grayson walked into the sunset with the capped-tooth, fake-boobs, uppity-southern bimbo. Tomorrow, she'd figure out how to say the words that somehow must be said.

Running her hands down the front of her dress, she smoothed out the fabric before heading out of the room. She'd just snapped the door closed behind her when she came face to face with the southern bimbo herself.

"Are you all right?" she drawled. "The festivities are about to start." Her smile was big, bright, and well-rehearsed. Her eyes, however, reflected her true feelings.

"Of course, I'm fine, just freshening up." Lexie didn't bother to fake a smile and stepped around Darla Mae.

"Lexie," Darla crooned from behind her, "I'm sorry your relationship with Grayson didn't last. I hope you were able to recognize his intentions early enough to avoid a broken heart."

Whipping around, Lexie narrowed her eyes and fought to move her retort past the lump in her throat.

With a syrupy smile plastered across her face, Darla Mae stepped closer to her. "Grayson and I were fated to be together. Although I'm sure you believed you were different, every fling he's ever had always brought him back to me. I can't help but feel partially responsible for your pain."

Lexie fought the urge to slap the look of pity she wore on her perfectly made-up face. "Every fling? Are you insinuating that our relationship meant nothing, and that the woman he'd once planned to marry was also nothing? Both she and I were just a momentary lapse in judgment?" Lexie wanted to sound accusing, unaffected by Darla Mae's bravado, but she knew her insecurities were showing, and her attempt to put this woman in her place had instead, become a line of questions she really wanted answered.

Darla Mae's condescending sigh vibrated down the empty hallway. "Is that what he told you? That he'd planned to marry that nothing dancer?" She frowned and shook her head. "She was simply a distraction for him, a part of his rebellion against his parent's expectations."

Lexie shook her head, wanting to scream that she was a liar, but deep down afraid she wasn't.

Darla Mae looked her directly in the eye and took another step forward. "He was never going to marry her. Or you for that matter. Why would he continuously return to me if he was serious about either of you?"

Advancing, Darla Mae brought them nose to nose and looked down at her. "No man can fake the passion he showed me last night. You don't really believe that he simply went home alone after pouring you, drunk and disheveled, into your own bed, do you?"

Lexie felt as if she'd been slapped. She struggled to recall the night before. Pieces of time floated through her mind, a kaleidoscope constantly turning, but never coming together in a clear picture.

Darla Mae smirked, and shaking her head, stepped around a stunned Lexie and gracefully descended the stairs.

Chapter 25

After a lengthy talk with herself and a stern reminder about why she was here, Lexie made her way back into the reception area. She could, and would, get through the next few hours without falling apart. Today was not about her, or Grayson. It was Aimee and Mark's day and she would forget about her pain and embrace their joy. She could do this, she had too.

Ryan spotted her and raced toward her, his green eyes bright with excitement. "Mom, I get to sit at the big table with you and Grayson." He was out of breath, and panting his words. "I can't get out of this monkey clothes yet though."

She couldn't help but laugh. "Do you mean monkey suit?"

Ryan nodded his head with vigor. "Grayson says that we have to stay in these monkey clothes till we get home, but that we can take off our coat and ties after everyone has emptied the champagne and starts dancing like fools." He grabbed her hand and started pulling her toward the table. "Come on, Mom, you get to sit with Grayson and me."

She felt Grayson's eyes on her as she was physically dragged to his side. Reading the place cards set neatly behind the plates on the table she knew she couldn't get out of this situation without causing a scene. She wished Ryan was wrong and they could change out of their monkey suits. Grayson looked too much like a groom as he stood there sipping a glass of champagne. He looked the way she'd dreamt he would; only she'd pictured herself in the white dress, and him smiling at the altar. But in her dream he didn't look uncomfortable and his eyes hadn't been pleading for understanding.

What did he think would happen when he showed up with Darla Mae at their friend's wedding? He was in for a surprise if he thought he could jump from her to another and be welcomed back again. She knew she'd been unfair with her silence, but once she'd gathered the courage to tell him the truth, he would have understood. Wouldn't he? She was no longer sure. Being honest with herself, she was no longer sure about anything between the two of them.

Gazing his way, she dipped her head in silent greeting and sat in the seat beside him. Other members of the party filtered in and took their seats, their chatter making the silence between the two of them obvious, and much more uncomfortable. Ryan couldn't sit still and seemed to talk to everyone at once as he bounced eagerly on his chair.

Focusing her attention to the newly married couple standing on the dance floor, she concentrated on forgetting Grayson was sitting directly beside her, or that his leg was burning a path of heat through her dress as it brushed her thigh.

The couple thanked everyone for coming, instructed the waiters to pour more champagne and announced that dinner would be served in less than ten minutes. When they exited the dance floor area, they made their way over to Lexie and Grayson, pausing in front of them.

"We are so grateful that you two stood up with us today. It wouldn't have been the same without you." Aimee's genuine smile was infectious.

"I wouldn't have missed it for the world," Lexie said honestly. "I know you two will have a long and happy life together."

"Marcus Lee is married. I never thought I'd see the day," Grayson chuckled. "I'm not sure whether to congratulate you Aimee, or give you my condolences."

Mark laughed and leaned over to kiss his bride. "Definitely your condolence, the poor girl has no idea what she's done."

Her smile permanently embedded on her face, Aimee playfully slapped at Mark. "I know exactly what I've done, and I won't regret one moment for the rest of my life."

Watching the two of them it was almost impossible to remember a time they weren't so obviously committed to each other. Lexie knew that secrets could be forgiven, she was witnessing that now, but her situation was different. Wasn't it? She sipped her champagne and glanced at Grayson. He was all smiles as he chatted with Mark, reminiscing about their college years when they'd been roommates. But his smile didn't reach his eyes.

The newlyweds took their seats at the center of the table as dinner was served. The conversation flowed loudly around them as Lexie sat in silence listening to her son list off the names of the constellations he'd discovered with his telescope. Grayson kept up with him, mentioning other stars Ryan should locate and explaining the general area in the sky where he should look.

Darla Mae sat at a table directly to the left of them, and nodded politely at the man beside her, never taking her eyes off Grayson.

After the toasts, the slicing of the cake, and the couple's first dance, the guests began to filter onto the dance floor. The music picked up its tempo and Lexie grabbed Ryan's hand, dragging him onto the floor. She noticed the moment she'd walked from behind the table, Darla Mae slid into her seat beside Grayson.

Returning from the dance floor, Lexie winced at the sight of Darla Mae whispering into Grayson's ear, her breasts rubbing against him as she leaned in, her bare arm draped comfortably over the back of his chair.

Ryan tugged on Grayson's sleeve and whispered something that made Grayson laugh. He nodded his head, and a huge grin spread across her son's face as Grayson untied Ryan's bow tie and slipped it off his neck, before Ryan raced back to the dance floor.

With Darla Mae on one side of Grayson and her son on the other, Lexie knew she was witnessing her biggest fear. Where was she in this picture? Would she be on the outside of a newly made family? Would Grayson move back to Kentucky and take Ryan with him?

Scenes, like previews in a movie theater, raced through her mind. Ryan begging to live with his father; Darla Mae, informing

Ryan that Lexie wasn't his mother, only a legalized babysitter; Grayson laughing at her when she told him Ryan was his son. Grayson admitting he knew about Ryan and not wanting him. Replaced, rejected, and enraged—she felt all of those things.

Needing an outlet, she walked to Darla Mae with a purposeful stride. "No wonder you needed to sit down. Your feet must be killing you in those hooker heels." Lexie snapped.

Darla Mae glared at her, turned back to Grayson, pasted a smile on her face, and said, "Oh, I'm sorry, I'm in your seat aren't I?" She stood and waved her arm over the chair like a game show hostess and stepped back.

Taking her seat, Lexie focused her attention on Luther, Aimee's best friend, as he shared his opinions of Darla Mae under his breath.

"She's got nothing on you girl. Don't waste another minute worrying about that tramp." Luther narrowed his eyes as he watched Darla Mae hovering behind Grayson. "She's got claws under those manicured nails. Grayson isn't a fool, he sees that."

"Thanks Luther, but you're giving Grayson too much credit," Lexie shrugged her shoulders.

Luther winked and leaned back in his chair. "I've been contemplating getting a bit of nip and tuck work done. Could I get the name of your plastic surgeon, Darla Mae?"

Lexie bent her head down trying to hide her laughter as Darla Mae stuck her nose in the air and stomped away.

"Luther, you're terrible," she giggled, "I love that about you."

Pulling his shoulders back, he smiled proudly. "I do what I can."

Grayson didn't seem as entertained. His disapproval was written clearly on his face. Aimee shook her head and tried to dislodge the visual of Darla Mae with Grayson from her mind. Part of her wished she'd never been told. Now she was dissecting every whisper, every touch, every look, and driving herself crazy.

Lexie startled when Grayson reached over and laid his hand tentatively on her leg. She shot up and glared at him. Through clenched teeth she instructed, "Don't."

He lurched back as if she'd slapped him.

Standing up, Lexie excused herself and walked out of the reception area. Following a brick pathway, lit by candles and torches, she entered a small seating area surrounded by hundreds of rose bushes. The scent was intoxicating, the flowers beautiful, and the area itself was exceptionally peaceful.

She jumped at the sound of her name. She'd been so focused on the gentle peach colored rosebud that she hadn't seen Emily sitting quietly on one of the cushioned chairs set around a small table.

"Are you okay?" Emily asked, her caring face slowly melted the last traces of Lexie's resolve.

"Can I ask you something?" Lexie sat beside Emily and studied her hands folded in her lap.

Emily nodded.

"If you'd have found Aimee when she was four, five, or even six, would you have brought her home? Removing her from the only parents she'd ever known?"

Looking shocked by the question, Emily cleared her throat and pulled Lexie's hand into hers. "That woman kidnapped her, Lexie. She took her out of my arms a day after she was born." Her eyes welled with unshed tears. "I missed her growing up, I missed all her firsts. I would give anything to have that time back."

Lexie gazed into Emily's eyes. "What about the woman's husband, the man Aimee believed to be her father? He didn't know Aimee wasn't his daughter. He was a victim like you were. His wife lied to him."

Emily grew silent, her head tilted back as she looked at the night sky. Without looking down she added, "He loved her completely, and she him." She wiped a tear from her cheek. "I'd like to believe I'd do the right thing. That I would put Aimee's needs before mine, but the truth is, I don't know if I would have believed anything they told me back then. I also can't forget that Aimee will never have a chance to know her real father. Or that Nathan died without knowing her."

Lexie simply nodded her head.

"Do you want to talk about it?" Emily asked.

"Desperately, but I need to talk to someone else first." Lexie hugged her friend and headed back to the reception.

The crowd had started to thin and those left were mainly on the dance floor. She spotted Grayson, his back to her, dancing with Darla Mae. As he held her against him, Darla Mae leaned closer, and slowly ran her hand down the middle of his back.

Pressure built behind her eyes and she quickly turned away before the tears began. Lifting a sleepy Ryan into her arms, she said her goodbyes to Aimee and Mark and walked away.

Chapter 26

The group was in high spirits as they gathered around the table overlooking the water—except for Lexie. She always looked forward to a Sunday afternoon at her parents' house, but today, she couldn't get the picture of Darla Mae and Grayson out of her head, or keep the words from Maggie's journal from replaying like an old scratched record. Worse, she couldn't shake the sense of loss that overwhelmed her.

Lexie's friends always had a seat at her parents table. The Waynes had a way of opening their arms that made it irresistible to stand outside their embrace. She gazed over at the chair Maggie had occupied on Sundays, and felt its emptiness stronger today. She couldn't help but see the irony in the fact that the empty chair beside Maggie's had been where Grayson sat only weeks ago. But today, he was absent from the Sunday gatherings, too. She watched her mother, her face aglow with happiness, as Ryan bounced with excitement on her lap. Her father reached over and tousled Ryan's hair without taking his attention from the story Marissa was telling him.

Marissa had been a part of the Wayne family forever, it seemed to Lexie. With her husband gone for business more than he was home, she'd was almost always present on Sundays, holidays, or any occasion the Waynes invented to get their children over to the house.

Lexie watched her brother's face as he listened to the conversation going on between Marissa and their father. Jordan had been in love with Marissa since high school. She'd been his first kiss and his first broken heart when she met Steve at college, and married him within six months. Sadly, Lexie knew that Marissa wasn't happy in her marriage. Over the nine years they'd been married, Steve had changed his mind about starting a family, and spent most of his time in the city. Marissa had spent the last four Christmases and Thanksgivings with her, instead of with her husband, and the family she'd always yearned for.

"Marissa, when are you going to give me another grandbaby? If I have to wait on these two to get married before I get another one, I'll be six feet under first." Betty never missed an opportunity to steer the conversation back to the topics she felt most important.

Her family was honest, loving, and warm, but to Lexie's dismay, they were also nosey, opinionated, and intrusive. Marissa may not have been born into the family, but she was a part of it, and that meant she was also subject to Betty's scrutiny as well as her demand for more grandchildren.

Somewhere in span of time Lexie's mind had wandered, the conversation had turned to Grayson, or his absence to be exact. She realized that everyone was staring at her, waiting for her to respond to a question she hadn't heard.

Marissa slid in, trying to defuse the onslaught they all knew was coming. "I think they are just trying to get to know each other better before the sounds of wedding bells ring in their future."

Betty was famous for her interrogations about a husband for Lexie, and picking a wife for Jordan. Lexie knew Betty wanted the same wife for Jordan that he wanted for himself, but unhappy or not, Marissa took her vows seriously.

Jordan looked over at Lexie, rolled his eyes, and sighed with tremendous exaggeration. His actions only fueled their mothers fire, and Betty began her rant of how she wasn't getting any younger, and neither were they. Lexie was sure her mother rehearsed for this day the entire week leading up to their visits.

Ignoring Marissa's attempt to steer the conversation in another direction, Betty locked onto Lexie. "Alexis Rae, it's time you settled down. You're lucky Grayson wants you. You're never going to get another man to stay for long with that sassy mouth of yours. You finally have a great man who's crazy about you, and you've changed your mind already. You can't run forever. Grayson has the patience of a saint to put up with you and you're just going to let him get away?"

As Betty continued with her outburst, Lexie laid her head on Marissa's shoulder and making a dramatic crying sound pleaded, "Please make it stop. Shoot me now." Marissa leaned over and placed her arm around her in mocking support.

As the afternoon wore on, the men eventually took their beers and moved from the table to the lounge chairs in the sand.

Inside, the women were working together clearing the dishes and putting away the leftovers. Conversation was once again on Lexie's inability to commit for the sake of her own happiness.

"I don't understand it. You're beautiful, intelligent and successful. It saddens me that you can't find one man who could make you happy. Besides, Ryan loves him, which should count for something." Betty *tsked* accusingly.

"Mom, enough already! Jordan is single and two years older than I am, why aren't you out there pestering him?" Lexie recognized that she sounded like a whiny three-year-old. She wasn't sure how to tell her mother the truth about Grayson. Maybe because she wasn't sure exactly what the truth was. Her eyes threatened to spill the tears she was fighting back.

"Lexie, we know why Jordan is single. There is no reason for me to worry about him being alone forever." Betty said.

"Why is Jordan single?" Marissa asked.

Lexie shook her head at her friend's naivety but said nothing.

Betty's head snapped up. She studied Marissa as if finally realizing that she was clueless as to her son's feelings for her. "Jordan is just waiting for the girl of his dreams. It's just a matter of time." Betty snapped the lid closed on the potato salad and slid the bowl into the refrigerator. Digging into the cupboard for another container, she continued. "Now Lexie, on the other hand, is the one I worry about." She straightened and looked into Lexie's face, her eyes radiating with sadness. "After Kyle died, I was sure she'd never love again. Watching her with Grayson, I know differently now. My confusion is why she is pushing him away."

Lexie looked down, not wanting her mother to see the pain in her eyes at the mention of his name. She could feel the heat of Marissa's gaze as it locked onto her.

"It's more complicated than that," Marissa whispered. "Lexie has learned some things about Grayson recently."

Lexie's head shot up. She eyed her friend, who stood still, wringing a hand towel with shaky hands. Looking up, Marissa gave Lexie a sheepish, innocent look and shrugged her shoulders.

Lexie narrowed her eyes into challenging slits, pursed her lips, and mimed the removal of an imaginary knife from her back.

"What does she mean, Lexie?" Betty leaned against the counter, her large brown eyes conveyed concern.

"Tell her Lex," Marissa prompted. "Maybe she can help." Rubbing Lexie's shoulder, Marissa picked up her water bottle and headed outside.

Walking around the counter, Betty climbed onto the stool beside her daughter and waited quietly. Lexie sat down beside her, and struggled for the right words to explain her situation.

"I…" Lexie looked into her lap, and chewed on her bottom lip. "Grayson…"

Betty reached over and took hold of her daughter's hand. "What is it, what happened?"

"I…" Lexie paused, swallowed, and wiped the tears from her cheek. "Mom, Grayson is Ryan's father."

Betty gasped, her mouth open, her eyes confused. "Why would you think that?"

Lexie inhaled a breath and let it out slowly. Turning to her mother, she explained the photograph, and reading Maggie's journal.

"You haven't talked to him since that night?" Betty asked, sounding troubled.

Shaking her head, Lexie leaned forward and laid her head against her mother's shoulder, needing her comfort.

Betty ran her hand over her daughter's hair. "You have to talk to him, and if you're sure, you have to tell him about Ryan."

She knew her mother was right, but her fear of the unanswered questions was paralyzing.

"Maggie thought he was dead," Lexie whispered. "What kind of man would let the woman he'd loved believe he had died?"

"You said Maggie hadn't told him she was sick, right?" Betty asked, her eyes glancing upwards as she searched through the pieces of the puzzle.

Lexie nodded her head. "But even if he thought she'd just walked away from him, what justification would that be? That's one hell of a heartless way to get revenge."

"I don't know him as well as you do, Lex, but it just doesn't sound like him."

"What if he knew about Ryan? What if he came back here to take him from me?" Lexie's voice cracked.

"If he did, why would he pursue you on a personal level? He would win in court if he's the biological father." Betty crossed her arms across her chest as if comforting herself. "You don't think he'll take Ryan away from us, do you?"

Tears streamed down Lexie's cheeks. Unable to speak over the lump in her throat she shrugged.

"I'm beginning to understand your frustration. None of this makes a lot of sense, and it's much more complicated now that you're in love with him."

"No! I'm not!" Lexie snapped.

Betty grunted and rolled her eyes.

"I can't be, Mom, I won't be! This is too much. It's too hard." Lexie stood up and tugged her purse strap onto her shoulder.

Betty slipped her arms around her daughter and pulling her close, she whispered into her ear, "Doesn't change the fact that you are."

"That would make me a fool." Lexie stepped back and called out to Ryan that it was time to go. Looking back at her mother she added, "I won't be a fool."

"Talk to him, Lexie. Don't make any rash decisions right now." Betty advised, scooping her grandson into her arms as he bolted into the kitchen from the back yard.

"Look, Grandma, I drew this," he bragged.

Tilting her head back to get a clear view, Betty smiled. Lexie looked over her mother's shoulder at the stick figures standing on either side of a policeman wearing a red cape. She recognized immediately that one of the figures was her and the other one was Ryan.

"It's beautiful, Ryan, really beautiful." Betty cooed, and pointing to the superhero policeman asked, "Is that Uncle Jordan?"

"No, it's Grayson." Ryan said, pushing out of her arms. "I miss him a lot, but Mom won't let me see him anymore." His green eyes pooled with tears. "She's mad at him. He made her cry."

Lexie turned her back so her son wouldn't see she was crying again.

Chapter 27

The fog was dense, gloomy, and matched her mood perfectly. It was also blocking her view of the ocean. Lexie pulled her sweater tighter against her chest and leaned back, closed her eyes and listened to the calming crash of the waves. She hadn't been able to sleep and finally gave up the attempt around three in the morning. Now, close to five-thirty, she prayed for the sun to break through and lift her mood along with the fog.

The weekend had been an emotional rollercoaster, and she felt drained. Her arms felt like lead when she tried to lift them, her legs like jelly. She couldn't eat, sleep, or concentrate. It'd gotten so bad that she'd even called her mother into to open the coffee shop, without any thought of the questions that would arise from it.

Marissa was coming to pick up Ryan at eight; it was time for her to face Grayson. The thought of it made her want to crawl back under the covers and hide. She had no idea what she was going to say to him, no words she came up with made sense. If they didn't make sense to her, how was she going to explain this to him? "Grayson, I'm not sure if you know this but Ryan is your son." Or, "Grayson, if I tell you Ryan is your son will you take him away from me, move to Kentucky and raise him with the southern bimbo?"

Sighing, she stood from the chair on the balcony and walked inside. The scent of coffee wafted through the house and her mouth salivated in expectation. She poured herself a cup and turned on the morning news, curling up on the couch.

The lead story was the wedding of Emily Sinclair's long lost daughter and her marriage to Marcus Lee over the weekend. There was footage taken from helicopters that had flown overhead during the reception, but very little else as the security staff had kept the photographers at bay.

She reached for the remote to change the channel, when a camera zoomed in on Grayson leaving the reception with Darla

Mae Pruitt. He held open the door to a car she didn't recognize and before climbing inside, Darla Mae cupped his neck and kissed him.

Lexie felt the wind expel from her lungs. She hadn't wanted to believe when Darla Mae told her she'd been with Grayson, but watching them on the morning news was impossible to ignore. Clicking off the television, she pulled her knees to her chest and rested her forehead against them.

"Mommy, are you sad?" asked a sleepy voice.

"Good morning, sweet boy," she pulled him onto her lap and cuddled him against her. "I'm not sad, just a little tired," she lied.

Concentrating on breathing evenly and not letting the tears fall, Lexie rested her cheek atop her son's head. She didn't think she could survive if Grayson tried to take him away from her. Ryan was her life now, and she'd promised to take care of him. Again, the thought of not telling Grayson her discovery ran through her mind.

Ryan shifted, still content to snuggle against her, and picking up the remote, turned the television back on and flipped it to his favorite cartoon channel. She sat with him, gently stroking his silken hair, enjoying the quiet connection between them, until Ryan decided he was "starving to death."

Settling on the stool in the kitchen, Ryan drank milk from a Disney cup and chatted about his plans for the day while Lexie cooked him pancakes. The routine felt different today. Part of her wanted to etch this moment into her mind, to ensure not a moment would be forgotten. Another part of her knew she would fight like hell to have these instants continue for the rest of her life.

After eating five pancakes, Ryan ran off to get dressed and Lexie cleaned the kitchen. When Marissa arrived, Lexie poured her a cup of coffee and sat beside her at the counter.

"You look like hell," Marissa pointed out.

"Gee, thanks," Lexie tried to chuckle, but couldn't make the sound.

"Are you nervous?" Marissa looked at her intently. "Do you know what you're going to say?"

"Yes and no," Lexie replied, sipping from her mug. "I don't think I can do this. What if he takes Ryan from me and runs back to Kentucky to raise my son with that she-devil?"

Marissa cracked a smile, shook her head, and then turned to her friend and said in a no nonsense tone, "You have to do this. You *need* to do this." She placed her hand over Lexie's in comfort. "I know it's hard, but it's right. Try to put the shoe on the other foot. If Ryan was your son and Grayson knew and didn't tell you because he was unsure of what would happen next, would that be fair to you or to Ryan? No, it wouldn't." Marissa answered her own question.

"Grayson isn't some stranger, Lexie, you know him. He knows you. Do you really think he would just thank you for the information and tell you to have Ryan packed and ready to move out after dinner?"

Lexie shook her head, but the tear that ran down her cheek portrayed her fear.

"You two can work this out. You love each other, and you both love Ryan. This could be a great thing for both of you."

"He doesn't love me," Lexie sobbed. "He's already out fooling around with that southern gutter rat. I didn't want to believe it, but they were kissing on the damn news this morning!" Lexie reached for a napkin and wiped her eyes. "I can't let that tramp raise my son. I won't do it! I promised to protect him, and if I have to pack up and move and change our names, that's what I'll do." She could feel the heat creeping onto her cheeks. She preferred the hot anger she felt now over the scared hopelessness from a moment ago.

"We're moving?" Ryan asked from the doorway, causing both women to jerk around, startled.

Lexie could see the fear in his eyes. "No sweetie, we're not moving. Mommy was just joking with Marissa." She knew her excuse sounded lame, but she'd drawn up blank in her quick search for a response.

"That's not a funny joke, Mom, and jokes are supposed to be funny. You should have Grayson tell some to you, his are super funny." She knew the crisis had been averted when he threw the strap of his backpack over his shoulder and pulled Marissa's hand to lead her to the door. "Come on," he prodded, "we've gotta get this show on the road." He paused, his face crinkling in thought. "What does that mean anyway?" He shrugged his shoulders and continued to propel Marissa out of the house.

"Hang on a second, Speedy," Lexie called after him. "Aren't you forgetting something?"

With an exaggerated eye roll, Ryan sauntered back to where she stood in the doorway. She crouched down to his eye level. "Sorry, Mom," he mumbled, and reached his arms around her neck to give her a hug and a kiss.

She smiled at him, stood and looked intently at her friend. "What if we're wrong?" She whispered, panic threatening to overwhelm her.

"We're not," Marissa reassured her. "If you start to back out, I want you to think about Emily Sinclair. Would you want Grayson to go through life not knowing?"

"That was below the belt," Lexie replied, recalling her friend's hopelessness as she searched for her only child for twenty-eight years. She also realized that Marissa's message stemmed from love. "I'll tell him, I promise."

"Maaaariiiiisssssssa," her son chimed from the porch.

"Coming," she yelled after him, then turning back to Lexie, whispered, "We need to talk about this southern bimbo and what you know or think you know. Have a bottle of wine chilled when I bring Ryan home."

With a final hug and wink from Marissa, and a wave from Ryan, Lexie shut the door behind them and leaned against the solid wood. She was petrified. And worse, she still had no idea what she'd say or how she'd say it.

Chapter 28

Monday morning didn't appear as if it were going to be any better than the previous mornings. Grayson had woken alone, with no word from Lexie—again. All of his calls had gone unanswered. She'd disappeared from the wedding without a word, and he still hadn't been able to get the vision of her standing under the arbor holding a bouquet of flowers out of his mind. If she weren't so mad at him, he would have walked across the aisle and kissed her right then and there. But she was mad at him, and thanks to Darla Mae, it didn't look like she would get over it any time soon. He just wished he knew why.

He turned on the morning news and walked into the kitchen for another cup of coffee. He hated that he was making his own again. He missed the perfect way Lexie made his coffee at the shop. With half an ear he listened to the story of a hotel fire, the latest steroid accusation of a major baseball player, and the traffic back up on Highway 1. Walking back to the living room, he stopped to open the shades, and looked out at the thick gray fog that hadn't yet burnt off. Taking a sip from his mug, he sat on the couch and kicked his feet onto the coffee table.

Hot coffee burned through his jeans, and he leapt off the couch holding his mug away from himself with one hand and brushing the scalding liquid from his legs with the other. His eyes never left the television screen. Big as life, on the morning news, was Darla Mae wrapped around him in what appeared to be a very intimate kiss. He groaned.

Why had they not continued to film the next fifteen seconds when he'd pushed her away and slammed the door behind her? At the time, he'd wondered what had possessed her to be so bold, but now he understood. She'd seen the cameras and wanted Lexie to see the footage. The blood rushed from his face as panic set in. Had Lexie seen the news? Would she believe he'd actually kissed another woman just hours after reminding her how much he loved her? Of course she would, it was in living color on the damn news.

He plopped back onto the couch and rubbed his eyes with the palms of his hands. He had to go see her, to explain what really happened, but he didn't want to make a scene at the shop. And if he knew Lexie, there was definitely going to be a scene. The question was what was the best way to corner her and force her to listen without being in the vicinity of sharp objects or having the entire town, or worse, Ryan present?

He changed his jeans, gathered his wallet and keys, and threw open the door in a rush to get to Lexie, when he collided with her outside his front door. God, she was beautiful.

"We've got to stop running into each other this way," he said lightly, hoping she would laugh, or smile. She didn't.

Watching her, waiting for her to say something, anything, he noticed her eyes were swollen, and she had dark circles beneath them. She looked frightened, sad, lost, and somehow lonely. Seeing her this way broke his heart. He knew it wasn't simply the news footage of Darla Mae, because the veins weren't throbbing in her temples, and she appeared to be without a weapon of any kind.

"Would you like to come in?" he finally asked, stepping back inside.

"I can come back," she said, stepping back. If he didn't know any better, she almost seemed frightened. Of him? It didn't make sense.

"Why would you do that? What's wrong with now?" He watched her, silently willing her to look up at him.

"Well, you were just leaving, I don't want to interrupt. I can come back later." She turned to go.

Panic surged through him as he stared at her slowly retreating back. Without a thought, he dropped his keys and his helmet, and reaching out, clutched her shoulders and turned her around.

"I was coming to find you, Lexie. Please talk to me," he pleaded.

She looked up, mutely watching him, a million internal thoughts flashing in her expressive eyes. None of them clear, and none of them reducing the dread that settled in his stomach. Brushing past him, she set her purse on the table and sat down at one of the dining room chairs. He hadn't sat at the table yet, and he'd pictured the first time with her much differently. Candles, wine, and dinner; definitely not Lexie's head bent down, clutching a book of some sort tightly against her chest and unable to make eye contact with him.

She still hadn't spoken and the air around them seemed to close in, filled with tension, fear, and sadness. Sitting down on the chair beside her he fidgeted with an imaginary piece of string on his jeans unsure of what to do with his hands. He yearned to bury them in her hair, to pull her onto his lap and kiss the sorrow from her eyes.

"Lex, about Darla Mae…"

Her eyes flashed with rage, and he felt guilty about the feeling of relief that washed over him. Rage, he could handle, her sadness, her distance, whatever this was, frightened him.

"I didn't come here to discuss your relationship with Darla Mae. I could really care less what you do with your free time," Lexie snapped, her words were angry, but Grayson could see the pain in her eyes.

"I don't have a relationship—" he began, but she immediately cut him off.

"Grayson, enough." The anguish in her eyes left him speechless.

"Lexie…" his voice trailed off. He couldn't find the words he wanted to say. To tell her how he felt about her.

Tears rolled down her cheeks as she set the book she'd been tightly clutching against her chest onto the table.

"I didn't come here to talk about you and me, at least not directly." She took a deep breath and lowered her eyes to her lap.

"It's…" Her voice hitched, then grew silent.

"Lexie, what is it? You're really scaring me." Grayson leaned forward and tried to take her hand.

She jerked it back like she'd been stung. "I don't know how to say this…"

"You can tell me anything." Grayson urged.

Looking up into his face as tears poured down hers, she whispered, "I think Ryan is your son."

Trying to process what she said, he started to laugh, assuming she was making a joke. "Lexie, unless there have been changes made in the last few years, I believe it takes more than six months to have a child together, let alone a four-year-old." He looked at her, wondering why she still appeared so somber. "And if you're trying to get me to marry you, I believe the proper way to trap a man is to tell him you're pregnant first."

When she still didn't laugh, he grew silent, watching her. She wasn't making any sense. She reached for the book on the table and pulled it onto her lap, stroking the cover.

"What is that?" he asked, gesturing toward the book.

"Ryan was adopted," she said, not looking up.

"Yes, I know that," he replied confused. "You told me already, and you know he means the world to me. It doesn't matter to me if he's yours by birth or by heart." Assuming her sudden retreat had something to do with her son, he attempted to reassure her. "I knew you were a mother when we met, Lexie. If I've done anything to cause you to believe that I wasn't in this for the long haul, I'm sorry. I love Ryan. I love you." He ran his hands through his hair, struggling to find the perfect words. "I see you both in my life, and I was hoping you saw me in both of yours as well. I know Darla Mae, crazy as she is, has convinced herself that she and I will be together, but I hope you believe—"

"Enough with Darla Mae!" she shouted, pushing back from the table, and pacing back and forth. She turned to him, tears flowing down her cheeks.

He opened his mouth to speak, and snapped it closed when he saw the look on her face.

"Grayson, my friend that died three years ago, her name was Maggie." Lexie said, appearing to search for a reaction from him.

"Ok?" he finally said, still unsure where she was going with this conversation.

"Maggie was Ryan's mother," she said, bobbing her head at him.

"I got that," he replied, still as confused as when she'd started.

"I believe she was *your* Maggie." Lexie slunk back into the chair like the effort to say the sentence had exhausted her.

"I don't…" Grayson shook his head trying to clear the muddled feeling. "What do you mean she was *my* Maggie?"

Lexie looked him directly in the eye and whispered, "Ryan Hunter. My son's name is Ryan Hunter. His mother was Margaret Austin."

Grayson shot out of the chair, sending it scattering across the floor. His voice was louder than he intended, "Maggie? Ryan?" His heart was pounding hard enough to exit his chest if he removed his hand. His knees wobbled and tears burned behind his eyes. "She wouldn't do that. It's not true."

Lexie took his hand, and wrapped his fingers around the book she'd been clutching. "She thought you were dead, remember?"

He shook his head, unable to speak.

"Read this. It's Maggie's."

Grayson didn't hear Lexie leave.

Chapter 29

The road signs came into view of the windshield and raced past in constant repetition. Lexie didn't know where she was headed; she just knew she wasn't ready to go home. The look of agony on Grayson's face would be forever etched in her mind. She couldn't recall seeing that much pain in anyone's eyes, at least outside of the hospice house.

Watching his reaction, she knew she'd misjudged him. And she should have known better. It would be a rare kind of heartless to walk away from your child, and Grayson was anything but heartless. She'd seen him with Ryan, his gentleness, patience, and most importantly, his genuine affection. That was not a man who would ever turn his back on any child, let alone his own.

Was it her own fears that allowed her to wonder if he was capable of letting the woman he'd loved believe he was dead? That was the only explanation, wasn't it? Either that or she was a complete mistrusting, rotten judge of character. How could she have believed for a second that Grayson could ever do that? She didn't deserve a man like him, and he deserved better than her. The reality of her behaviors overwhelmed her, and she pulled the car to the shoulder of the road.

Laying her head against the steering wheel, she cried. She thought of Maggie, of Ryan, of Grayson, and even of herself, and slapped her palm against the dashboard in frustration. Her crying turned to sobbing, and her body wracked with the pressure. Unsure of how long she'd been parked on the side of the road, she was startled by a rap on the window.

A state patrol officer stood outside, looking at her strangely. She lowered the window and tried to paste a reassuring smile onto her face. She hadn't even noticed him pull up.

He looked at her, peeked into the back seat, and asked, "Ma'am, are you all right? Do you need some assistance?"

"I'm…" her voice caught in her throat. "I'm fine, thank you officer."

"Could I see your license and registration please?" he asked, still looking puzzled.

Reaching into the glove box, she caught sight of her reflection in the rear view mirror. She looked terrible. Streaks of black mascara ran down both cheeks, her eyes were swollen slits on her face, and the part of her eyes showing were bright red. She looked crazed, beaten, and exactly like she felt.

Embarrassed, she handed him her license and registration. "I'm having a rough day. I was just heading home."

Looking from her license to her, and back to her license, he finally pointed out, "You live the other direction."

"I was just turning around."

"Any relation to Jordan Wayne?" he asked.

"He's my brother," she replied, wishing the cop world wasn't so small. She knew she wouldn't get two miles before her brother received a call.

"Okay, Alexis Wayne, head on home, drive safely, and try to have a better day." He nodded his head and walked back to his car.

She waited for him to pull out, and turned her car back toward home.

An hour later, she pulled up at Marissa's and wasn't surprised to see her brother's cruiser parked in the driveway. He'd gotten the call all right, and he knew her well. Of course she wouldn't have gone home, she'd run to her friend if she was upset, and he'd need to see her for himself.

The front door flew open, and both of them came barreling toward her, yanking open her car door before she could pull the handle.

"What in the hell is going on?" Jordan barked, his tone harsh, but his eyes gentle and worried.

"Where's Ryan?" Lexie didn't want him to see her like this.

"Mom picked him up," Jordan replied, cutting off Marissa's attempt.

"Lex, are you okay?" Marissa stepped between them, and held out her hand.

The emotions began to surface again. What was it with best girlfriends or mothers that brought out the needy child in all women? Marissa pulled Lexie into her arms as she cried—again.

"Damn it! Would somebody tell me what the hell is going on?" Jordan squawked.

Marissa turned and scowled at him. "Jordan, wait inside. Lexie will tell you what is going on with her when she calms down, and only if she chooses to. You will not yell at her right now, do you understand me?"

Jordan nodded his head like a scolded child and walked inside as he'd been instructed.

Lexie collapsed into Marissa's arms again and cried, clinging to her. "You should've seen him," she mumbled into her shoulder. "He was distraught, stunned, almost like he was in shock." She stood upright, wiped her eyes and looked into her friend's concerned face. "How could I have thought he would've turned his back on Ryan? Or Maggie? How could I have doubted him?"

Marissa reached out, grabbed her by the arms, and shook her gently. "You didn't know. You didn't know what happened. Anyone would have questions, Lexie."

Lexie knew her friend was trying to help, to ease her guilt, but she knew how wrong she'd been. How unfair she'd been to Grayson. She let Marissa lead her inside, and gratefully accepted the Kleenex Jordan handed her.

"Lex," her brother said tenderly, "are you all right? What happened? I've never seen you like this before."

"I've made such a mess of things." Lexie rubbed her hands over her face.

Jordan sat beside Marissa on the couch across from Lexie and listened as she told him what she'd discovered about Maggie and Grayson. His mouth remained open in shock until she'd finished. It snapped closed long enough for him to mutter, "Oh shit, sis."

Chapter 30

Grayson snapped the book closed and set it on the table. He'd read it from front to back, four times, and was still struggling to comprehend what it meant. Maggie had loved him, in fact, she'd loved him so much she'd let him go when she'd needed him most because she thought it was the only way to keep him safe. So why was he so angry at her for that? He'd spent the last five years thinking he'd meant nothing to her, that he was disposable.

Rising from the couch, he stripped off his clothes, climbed into the shower and let the hot water run over his face. His eyes burned, his stomach knotted, and his head was foggy. It was all too much.

He had a son. He grabbed for the wall to balance himself when his knee's buckled. His breathing was ragged; he couldn't seem to pull enough air into his lungs. He'd spent the last six months getting to know a wonderful little boy, and today, he learned that same boy was his son. "My son. Ryan is my son." No matter how many times he said it out loud, he couldn't bring himself to fully believe it.

Switching off the water, he wrapped a towel around his waist, and walked to the sink. Using his hand, he wiped the condensation from the mirror. Leaning forward, he studied his reflection in the mirror. He ran his hands over his face, and recognized he needed a shave. His eyes were swollen, bloodshot, and dazed. Dark hair hung over his forehead, flipping up at the ends where the water had exposed his natural curls. The same curls as Ryan.

What did he do now? He'd loved two women in his life. Both of them had lied to him, misjudged him, and turned his world upside down. Had Maggie tried to reach him when she learned she was pregnant? If so, why hadn't the message reached him? How long had Lexie known Ryan was his son? Is that why she'd run away from him?

Shaking his head, he walked into the kitchen, tossed back two aspirin in an attempt to reduce the pounding in his head, left a message for Jordan that he was taking a few days off, and climbed into bed.

Three hours later, he gave up on sleep, dressed, and jumped on his motorcycle, driving it blindly through the night. The cool air felt good against his skin as he revved the throttle, picking up speed, winding around the curves of the highway. He could smell the salty scent of the ocean, and imagined the soft lull of the waves against the shore.

He'd lost track of time watching the white stripes of the highway race past him. The low fuel light came on, and he'd driven far enough north that rain was soaking through his jeans and t-shirt.

Pulling off the highway, he parked in front of a small truck stop diner with a flashing neon sign announcing it was open twenty-four hours. The diner was empty except for the cook seated at the counter flipping through a newspaper, and a heavyset waitress pouring salt into half empty shakers.

They both looked up when he walked inside. The aproned chef nodded and turned his attention back to his newspaper. The waitress looked over the top of the glasses perched on her nose, and smiled. "Can I get you some coffee, darlin'?"

Grayson nodded appreciatively, and sat in one of the booths. The waitress placed a steaming cup of coffee in front of him, pulled a pencil out of the orange bun atop her head, and flipped open a tablet to take his order. Looking at her nametag he said, "Just coffee, thank you, Opal."

"Don't take this the wrong way, sugar, but you look like you could use a hot meal." She tilted her head, studying him. "You could also use a friendly ear. Whatever's eating at you ain't small."

Grayson looked at her, and couldn't help but smile. "You decided all of that in under a minute? Do I look that bad?"

Opal reached over and pinched his cheek. "Nah, not bad, just… well, a bit lost." She wrote something on her tablet, and looked at him again. "I'm thinking a nice omelet with extra mushrooms, and a couple slices of sourdough toast. That oughta hold you for a bit." She winked at him and shouted at Lloyd to fire up the grill.

He sipped his coffee, and watched the rain fall in the single street light shining over the parking lot. It wasn't long before Opal set a gigantic omelet in front of him, topped off his coffee, and slid into the booth across from him.

She watched him in silence, almost as if she wasn't leaving until she was sure he'd eaten something. He indulged her and cut a large bite of his omelet. Nodding her approval, she slid out, poured another cup of coffee, and sat back down across from him. "Wanna talk about it?"

Something about her made him want to open up. Maybe that's what he needed, a stranger, with no preconceived notions, to help him figure out what he needed to do now. He leaned back, settled his arm over the top of the booth and shook his head.

"You'd never believe me if I told you," he told her.

"Try me," she challenged, sipping from the coffee she'd poured for herself.

"Ok, but don't say I didn't warn you." Grayson chuckled, and cleared his throat. "Five years ago I was in love with a woman."

"It always starts with a woman," Opal snickered at her own truth.

"The night before I was scheduled to deploy to Iraq, she broke it off with me, said she didn't love me anymore." He nodded at the scowl on Opal's face. "I never heard from her again, and six months ago, I fell in love again. She was a single mother with a wonderful little boy. She was strong headed, stubborn, loving, a great mother, beautiful."

"So why do you say 'was'?" Opal asked.

Grayson looked into his lap, unsure of how to explain this. "It has recently been brought to my attention that Ryan, that's the little boy, is actually my son."

Opal squinted and pursed her lips. "How does that work, sugar?"

With a sarcastic grunt, he continued. "The girl that broke it off with me was sick. She had cancer. And it seems that's why she left me. She didn't want me to be distracted with worry while I was at war."

"That was a very selfless thing she did."

He frowned. "But then she discovered she was pregnant with my son."

"Am I missing something here? I thought the woman you was lovin' now had your son?" Opal looked as confused as he felt.

"She does, and this is where it gets interesting." Grayson took another sip of his coffee. Opal was now leaning on both elbows against the table in anticipation. "Somehow, Maggie, that's the birth mother and my old love, believed I'd died in Iraq. I can't figure that one out. But she died when my son was only a few months old."

Opal's eyed welled with tears.

"Now, here's the craziest part. The woman I've been dating discovers that her friend who passed away and whose son she adopted is in fact, my ex, therefore making Ryan my son. Only I'm not dead."

Opal's mouth was agape, and her forehead scrunched in confusion.

"So what would you do if you were me?" Grayson asked seriously.

Opal started to laugh. Tears rolled down her cheeks, and she rocked back and forth. Her laughter continued for several minutes, boisterous and booming.

After several deep breaths, she finally managed to say, "You scoundrel! You actually had me going for a while there." She took another deep breath and looked at him seriously. "If you didn't want to talk about it, you could've just told me, sugar. I wasn't trying to force you or anything."

Grayson stood up, pulled a twenty from his wallet and laid it on the table. He leaned over and kissed Opal gently on the cheek and exited the diner without another word.

The truth was so farfetched, even Opal thought he'd made it up.

Chapter 31

It had been two weeks and three days since Lexie had heard from Grayson. She'd finally stopped leaving messages, but now she was beginning to panic. Once she'd gotten the vision of his crestfallen face out of her mind, she began to picture courtrooms, and restraining orders. These days she jumped when the phone rang, if there was a knock on her door, and even when a customer came through the door of the coffee shop. She was making herself crazy, and needed it to stop. She needed to talk to him, to find out what his intentions were, if he was all right.

It had been impulse that made her follow him when she spotted Grayson on his motorcycle at the stop light. She'd tried to stay behind him, and out of view, but sitting in her car watching him now, she felt like an intruder.

She wanted to put the car in reverse and leave him alone. Let him deal with the demons she could only imagine were haunting him. But the slump of his shoulders made her ache for him, and the thought of another two weeks of silence made her step out of the car.

She walked across the grass, following the familiar path, stepping around the tombstones of the cemetery. Grayson must have sensed her presence and whipped around, his face set in a grim mask. His growl couldn't mask the evidence of the tears on his lashes.

They silently watched each other, the tension between them thick and unfamiliar. Lexie reached out to touch him, and sucked in her breath when he shot back to avoid her hand. Lowering her head, she fought to control the hurt she was feeling from showing on her face.

"I've tried to call you," she finally managed, looking up at him.

His eyes were bluer than she remembered, and harder then she'd ever seen them. "I've been a bit distracted," he replied, his tone dismissive.

Lexie stood where she was, unsure of how to proceed with him. His shoulders were straight, his hands tucked stiffly into the pockets of his jeans. The wind blew through his hair, and carried the familiar scent of him straight to her heart.

"Grayson…" She still didn't know what to say, but she desperately wanted to hold him, to soothe his pain.

He turned around, his stance the same, his eyes direct and intimidating. "Have you told him?" She knew he was referring to Ryan and she shook her head. "I'd like to be there when you do," he stated, more of a command then a question.

"Okay," she nodded taking another step toward him.

Holding out his hand to stop her, he said, "I have three questions for you. I need you to be completely honest with me."

"Okay," she said again.

"Did you, even for a minute, wonder if I'd known of Maggie's pregnancy, and turned my back on them?" He watched her intently.

She hadn't anticipated the question, and was deadly afraid to answer it. She swallowed hard, "Well—"

He cut her off. "It's a simple yes or no question, Lexie. Did you or didn't you believe I was capable of ignoring my own son?"

Her eyes pleaded with him, and her hands began to sweat. "It's not as simple as that."

"Yes or no," he demanded clenching his jaw.

Tears slowly rolled down her cheeks and she nodded.

If it was possible, his eyes became even harder. "Did you ever question if I was capable of allowing Maggie to believe I'd died, if I were somehow behind her misconception?"

"Grayson, please understand…" the look on his face caused the words to fail her.

He turned and looked at Maggie's headstone in silence for a moment before turning and stepping toward her. His eyes narrowed, "How long have you known Ryan was mine?"

"Not long…um…" she could feel her panic rising.

"How long, Lexie?" He raised his voice. "When did you know?"

She stuttered, "I…I…found her picture in your drawer."

"When?" He repeated impatiently.

Beginning to sob, she looked down, needing to break his scrutiny. Grayson lifted her chin, forcing her to look up. His eyes were no longer harsh, but the sadness that now filled them made her answer ever harder. "The night we made love."

He simply nodded his head.

"Grayson, let me explain…" she begged.

"I would like to tell Ryan immediately, before he hears it anywhere else. Can I come by tomorrow?" he asked her quietly.

Neither of them had moved, yet the distance between them seemed insurmountable. She felt him slipping away, and realizing her betrayal, felt the desperation.

"Of course, I would like that very much," she smiled up at him, praying he could see the love she had for him.

"I won't stay long. Just long enough to make sure he's all right with all this." He stepped around her and began to walk away.

"Can you stay for a while after?" she asked, praying he'd say yes.

"There's no need," he answered matter of fact.

Stepping over to him, she reached for his arm to stop his retreat. "I thought maybe we could talk about us, and what happens now."

Removing her hand, he replied, "There is no us. The rest, as far as Ryan is concerned, we'll figure out as we need to."

She watched him walk across the grass, and over the crest of the hill. She sank to her knees in despair when she heard the roar of his motorcycle fade into the distance.

She leaned against her friend's headstone. "Oh Maggie, what have we done?"

Chapter 32

The following night, Grayson stood outside Lexie's condo, desperately trying to find the courage to knock on the door. Tonight everything would change. There was no turning back. Tonight he'd begin a relationship with his son, and be forced to explain to him that the three of them couldn't be a family.

How was he supposed to explain that to a four-year-old, when the thought of it made his heart ache? How was he supposed to raise his son with her, when he still loved her so much, knowing they couldn't be together? It all seemed so unfair. How did things get so messed up? He knew he had to walk away from her, it was the only option he had considering she had no faith in him. Not as a human being, and certainly not as a man.

In the past six months, he'd lost the only two women he'd ever loved. But he knew he needed to hold on tightly to the good he'd discovered as well. Tonight, he'd introduce himself to his son. Not as his friend, but as his father.

His stomach turned. He couldn't remember the last time he'd been so nervous. Wiping his hands on the front of his jeans, he cleared his throat and rang the doorbell.

Lexie opened the door, and he had to remind himself he was no longer free to scoop her into his arms. God, he wanted to. He wanted to talk about all of this with her, his discovery of Ryan, the truth about Maggie, even the heartache he felt over her.

Her eyes were free of makeup, swollen, and red. It was clear she'd been crying. He had to fight himself again as the urge to comfort her grew strong. Having just brushed past her, Ryan threw himself into Grayson's arms.

"I've been looking for ya," Ryan said, his eyes bright with pleasure. "I've missed you so much."

Grayson knelt down and his heart lurched when Ryan wrapped his arms around his neck, and squeezed. He smelled of soap and fabric softener, and Grayson clung to him, holding him tightly, not wanting to let him go.

"I've missed you too, buddy," Grayson told him, setting him back on his feet.

Ryan grabbed Grayson's hand and dragged him past Lexie and into the kitchen. "Mom showed me how to bake a pie. I flatted the crust. It's apple, want some?"

Not waiting for an answer, Ryan climbed onto the counter and pulled down three plates. He'd just reached for the knife when Lexie rushed in and placed her hand over his. "You know better," she scolded, but her eyes remained gentle.

Ryan mumbled his apology and again grabbed for Grayson's hand, leading him to the dining room table. "Mom said you've been doing person stuff. I'm glad you're back. I wasn't crying like Mom, but you were gone for a long time. I didn't like it."

Grayson's heart warmed knowing his son had missed him. But it ached knowing Lexie had been crying and Ryan had noticed. "I'm sorry I've been gone for so long." He reached out and patted Ryan's shoulder.

Lexie placed a slice of pie in front of each of them and a glass of milk for Ryan. She offered Grayson some coffee and walked back to pour herself a cup after he'd declined. He could tell by the slump of her shoulders she was struggling to hold herself together. This wouldn't be easy for either of them.

Taking a huge bite, Ryan smiled in delight. "Nummy, taste it," he prompted. He watched as Grayson took a bite and nodded his head in appreciation. "Mom did the hard part. She won't let me use the knife, keeps saying I'm too young, but I'm not."

Smiling at him, Grayson said, "It's only because she wants you to be safe. Knives can be very dangerous, even for adults."

Ryan grunted and took another bite as Lexie sat down at the table. Grayson could see her nerves in the restlessness of her body and the shaking of her hands. He still had no idea what to say, and catching her eye, silently implored who should tell him. She nodded her head toward him, and looked down into her coffee cup, the tension heavy between them.

Grayson gulped and took a deep breath. "Ryan, we have something to tell you." He searched for the words as his son looked at him with anticipation. Unable to find them, he looked over to Lexie for help only to find her still staring down. "Um…well…"

"What?" Ryan looked at Grayson, and back at his mother. "You're not leaving again, are you?" He looked terrified at the thought.

"No, it's nothing like that," Grayson reassured him. "In fact, I think it's pretty good news, and I hope you'll agree." He took another deep breath and looked into his son's curious face. "I'm… It turns out…um…Ryan, I'm your dad." The air expelled from his lungs in a strong release of pressure.

Ryan began to bounce in his chair, his smile stretching from ear to ear. Grayson felt a surge of relief at the delight on his son's face.

"I knew it!" Ryan exclaimed. "I prayed and prayed, and it worked!" He jumped from his chair and threw his arms around Grayson, almost knocking him backwards. Ryan then rounded the table and hugged his mother tightly. "Thank you," Ryan bellowed and flopped back into his chair. Breathless now, Ryan beamed at Grayson. "Can I be the head man, like you were?"

Lexie and Grayson both looked over the table at each other, confusion etched in their brows. Grayson spoke first, "The head man?"

"At the wedding," Ryan clarified. "Like you with Mark. I know I'm little, but I can do it. Please?" he begged.

"The wedding?" Lexie asked.

This time it was Ryan who looked perplexed. "Yeah, at yours and Grayson's wedding, I wanna be the head man."

Grayson's stomach pitched, and he felt the sting of tears behind his eyes. He looked over at Lexie and watched her wipe the tears from her cheeks. He felt like a heel. "Ryan, your mom and I aren't getting married."

"But you just said you're gonna be my dad," Ryan's bottom lip began to quiver.

Grayson stood up, lifted Ryan and sat back down with him on his lap. "No, I said I was your dad. I am your dad, really. I know this is all a bit confusing."

Ryan pushed off Grayson's lap and stood unsteadily before him. "So you're not marrying us?" Ryan burst into tears and rushed from the room when Grayson shook his head. They both jumped at the loud bang of his bedroom door slamming.

Leaning onto the table, Grayson rested his head against the palms of his hands. After a few moments of silence, he heard Lexie get up.

"I'll go talk to him," she said.

"Should I come too?" he asked her, unsure of the proper way to handle this.

"No, but will you wait?" Her eyes implored him. "He may need to talk to you as well after I explain things."

"Of course," he informed her before she disappeared down the hall.

Grayson rose and began to pace. Her home was familiar to him, but tonight felt like the first time he'd seen it. He stopped and looked at the framed photographs on a long table, studying each one. It was clear how happy Ryan was with Lexie. He wondered if there was room in their lives for him. Shaking his head, he mentally corrected himself, not in their lives, but in Ryan's. They couldn't be a family in the true sense of the word, but he hoped he and Lexie could come to an agreement of sorts to jointly raise Ryan.

He turned when he heard footsteps behind him. Ryan had tear stains down his cheeks, and his shoulders were hunched forward. Not exactly the reaction he'd had earlier, or the one Grayson desperately craved.

"Hi," Grayson said, kneeling down in front of him.

"So are you really my dad?" Ryan asked softly.

"It looks that way." Grayson reached out and rubbed Ryan's arm, searching for a way to touch him without yanking him into his arms like he wanted to do. "But I'd like to know how you feel about that."

"Okay, I guess," Ryan sniffled. "I just wanted us to live together, so we could watch the stars every night, and you could show me how to use a knife to cut apples."

Grayson looked over his head at Lexie, leaning against the doorframe. She was watching them intently, worry lines creased her forehead, and pools of tears glistened in her eyes. His eyes locked with hers, unable to find an answer to the questions between them. She'd hurt him. More than that, she'd betrayed him, and broken his heart with her lack of faith in him. He didn't see how they could come back from that.

"We'll buy a telescope for my house too, and you can have your own room there as well as here," Grayson told him in an attempt to reassure him.

Ryan nodded his head, and tears rolled down his cheeks. "Yeah," he said quietly.

Lexie stepped into the room and wrapped her arm around Ryan's shoulders. "It's time for bed, sweetie," she told him, protectively pulling him toward her.

"I'll see you soon, okay?" Grayson told him, standing up and ruffling the hair on the top of his head.

"Night," Ryan mumbled, allowing himself to be led back down the hallway.

Grayson poured himself a cup of coffee and sat down at the table to wait for Lexie. He saw her surprise when she came back into the room. "I thought we should talk," he told her.

She sat down in the seat across from him. "I think it's just going to take a while for him to fully comprehend all this." Her eyes, always so expressive, told him she would need time as well.

"We have a lot to work out, but for now, I only want what's best for Ryan," he assured her.

"I appreciate that," she replied.

Silence simmered between them, each lost in their own thoughts. Grayson felt his chest constrict, like the unmentioned elephant in the room had sat directly on his rib cage. He looked up at Lexie, desperate to hold her, yet angry at her that he couldn't.

"So what do we do now?" She asked.

"I have some business to deal with in Kentucky. I'd like to take Ryan with me for a few weeks, introduce him to my family, and spend some time with him." Grayson watched her, panic, fear, sadness, anger, all flashed across her face.

"Do you really think that's the smartest thing to do now?" she snapped. She covered her mouth, seeming surprised at her tone. "Sorry, I just meant, he's only now learned the truth. Isn't it a bit soon to introduce him to your family?"

"I don't think it is, and my trip can't wait." Grayson held her gaze. "I'd like my son to meet his grandparents, Lexie."

He recognized her beginning signs of anger. Her jaw clenched, her eyes sparked, and her shoulders straightened, causing her to sit a bit taller. "Are you telling me you're taking him with you, or asking me?"

"That depends on your point of view." Grayson stood from the table and placed his coffee mug in the sink. It wasn't wasted on either of them how familiar the act was or the hollowness of it now. "I'll pick him up the day after tomorrow," he informed her before letting himself out the front door.

Chapter 33

Grayson Hunter had some nerve, Lexie thought to herself as she turned the page of the magazine she'd brought for the plane ride to Kentucky. The look of shock on his face when she'd told him she'd be going as well had given her some joy, but it was short lived. The reality was she would be spending two weeks with a man who didn't want her, in a house full of strangers. She chose to ignore the fact Grayson's change of heart was mainly her fault. After all, he was the man with all the secrets. She allowed her anger to be all the justification she needed.

Then, of course, there was Darla Mae Pruitt. She mustn't forget she'd have the painful task of seeing that vulture hovering over Grayson for two straight weeks.

What else could she have done? Did he really think she would just let him load her son onto an airplane and fly off with him into the sunset? Somebody had to make sure her son would be returned to her, and preferably emotionally unscathed. They'd never been apart from each other and she'd be damned if she wouldn't be there for him when he could need her most.

She told herself it had nothing at all to do with the fact that she was determined not to let Darla Mae's claws become embedded in Grayson. Each time her mind went there, she convinced herself it had nothing to do with her, but everything to do with protecting Ryan. She couldn't allow her son to be raised by that manipulative harlot. Over her dead body, she thought, flipping the page in her magazine with such force the corner ripped off.

Grayson raised his head from the back of the seat and looked over at her, his eyebrow raised in question. She scowled at him and turned the page again, this time with exaggerated care. Ryan tugged at her, pointing excitedly out of the window as the plane cut through the clouds on its descent.

"Look, it's a mountain," he told them breathlessly.

Ryan spent the next forty-five minutes with his face pressed to the small round window of the plane. Lexie sat beside him delighted by his excitement, yet feeling her anxiety increase with each minute that passed. By the time they'd touched down, her stomach bubbled with such force she was certain she would be sick.

"I wouldn't have believed you were a nervous flyer," Grayson said, obviously noticing her discomfort.

She didn't respond, but she was grateful he'd believed it was the flying that had her feeling this way. After they'd unloaded from the plane, she slipped into the restroom to pull herself together. Staring at her reflection in the mirror, she was mortified to see she had the same green tinge as the Mr. Yuck stickers on her cleaning products.

Splashing water on her face, she leaned against the sink and took a couple of deep breaths. She was acting ridiculous. The part that bothered her most was that she wasn't sure exactly why. She could almost believe she was having a premonition of sorts, if she believed in that kind of thing.

"You're acting like a silly girl," she told her reflection in the mirror. "You're acting like you're going to discover dead bodies buried beneath their barn."

She jumped when she heard a giggle behind her. Turning, she realized she wasn't alone and had just been caught talking to herself in the mirror.

"Let me guess, first time meeting the in-laws?" The friendly woman rinsed her hands in the sink beside her. "It's not so bad. The nerves will settle, but don't have any dreams of being besties with the mother. That *never* happens."

Lexie opened her mouth to reply, but nothing made it past her tongue.

The stranger dried her hands and smiled before turning to leave. "Good luck."

The woman was right; it did kind of feel like she was meeting her in-laws for the first time. Only for her, it was after she'd divorced their son and dragged his heart over a mile of gravel. Maybe it was worse than that. She was meeting her son's grandparents for the first time, and ironically, they didn't yet know he existed. Worse, if they did know, they had chosen to pretend he didn't exist. She wondered if she would know the truth simply by witnessing the introduction.

When she stepped out of the bathroom, she spotted Grayson and Ryan standing at the tall windows, watching another plane take off. She couldn't make out what they were saying but Ryan was talking non-stop, his hands moving a mile a minute. Grayson reached over and put his arm around him, using his other hand to point at the plane just touching down. Her heart melted watching the two of them. It was the first time she realized how similar they were in both looks and mannerisms.

They turned when she walked up behind them, Ryan grinning widely, and Grayson seeming a bit awe-struck. She leaned over and whispered in Grayson's ear.

"You'd better get used to it. I can't get through a day without that little boy wrapping himself tighter around my heart."

He looked at her, with his heart in his eyes when Ryan took hold of his hand.

Leaning toward him again, she added, "Or at least until he's sixteen. From what I hear, after that the only thing wrapping tightly is your hand around a bottle of some kind, drinking the pain away and praying for the return of the non-possessed child you used to know." She laughed at the look of horror on his face, and added, "Or at least that's what my parents said happened to them."

Grayson shook his head. "That makes sense. Your parents must have saints named for them, after raising you and Jordan."

For a moment, it was almost like it used to be, the three of them, laughing, together, teasing each other and happy. But Lexie was reminded of where they were and why the minute the limousine pulled up to the curb at the airport. An older man wearing a black suit and black hat came around the car and opened the door. He directed the skycap to load their luggage into the trunk and turned to smile at Grayson.

"Welcome home, Grayson, sir," he said. Looking over at Lexie and Ryan standing behind him, his eyes showed his surprise before he added, "I was informed that you'd be bringing one guest. Shall I call ahead and have another room prepared for your additional guest?"

Another room prepared? Chauffer's, limousines and Grayson,sir? Lexie was beginning to feel like she'd stepped into a modern day version of *Gone with the Wind*. "That won't be necessary," she informed the chauffer. "My son and I will be fine in one room, thank you."

Ryan tugged on Grayson's sleeve, a mixture of excitement and trepidation playing across his face. When Grayson looked down at him, he asked, "Is this your car?"

"It's here to pick us up, yes," Grayson answered.

"Can I get in?" Ryan was inching his way closer to the open door. When Grayson told him yes, Ryan ran and jumped inside, causing all three of them to laugh at the number of "Wow's" and "you gotta see this" that were being shouted from behind the tinted windows.

The drive from the airport was beautiful. Pastures of deep green grass were surrounded by white fences, and horses ran happily through the fields. Tall yellowwood trees bordered portions of the road, creating a warm cocoon-like feeling. She couldn't remember having seen such a beautiful place.

The driver turned off the main road and through a large gate with Hunter Stables scrolled in the metal. The driveway seemed to go on for miles, and she could see acres and acres of pastures. They passed a huge barn with men walking horses in and out of the large open doorway.

The driveway curved again, and Lexie's mouth fell open when the house came into view. When Grayson had told her he'd grown up on a ranch, this was certainly not what she'd pictured. She counted four chimneys rising from the roof, and two huge covered porches granted a clear view of the property. Large trees created a beautiful green backdrop to the tan brick and white pillars of the mansion. The driveway circled around a huge bronze statue of a horse rearing up on its hind legs.

"Ranch, huh?" She mumbled, unaware she'd spoken aloud.

Grayson laughed, "Of sorts, yes."

"And you choose to live in a tiny one bedroom apartment and work for scraps as a cop." She shook her head. "Doesn't make a lot of sense to me."

"I'm doing what I love to do," he told her, looking directly into her eyes as if willing her to believe him. "This is my parent's world. It was never mine."

The driver stopped the limo at the base of the wide stairs that led to the massive front doors and came around the open the door. Before she could fully stand, the front doors opened and another man in a black suit came toward them. After greeting Grayson, he began to unload the bags from the trunk.

"Hello Grayson, darling."

Lexie looked up at a tall, striking woman with dark hair pulled back smoothly from her face. She wore charcoal gray slacks and a cream cashmere sweater with multiple strands of pearls falling in different lengths from around her neck. Her hands were folded in front of her with more pearls wrapped around her wrist and an enormous diamond ring caught the light of the sun. She looked at Lexie and Ryan with curiosity but didn't move to approach them.

"Hello, Mother," Grayson replied, stepping onto the porch and kissing her delicately on the cheek.

Lexie was surprised by the formality between them. There was no warmth, no signs of excitement at seeing each other after so long a time. The woman smiled, but it didn't reach her eyes and appeared well practiced.

Grayson turned to them and waved them over. "Mother, this is my friend Alexis Wayne."

Lexie held out her hand, only to have it ignored. "It's very nice to meet you," she said in a clipped voice. "And this is my son, Ryan." Lexie added.

Ryan stepped back, and took hold of his mother's hand. He looked up at Lexie, and she was surprised by the fear in his eyes. "Ryan, can you say hello to Grayson's mother?" Lexie nudged him slightly.

Ryan watched her warily but did as he was asked. "It's nice to meet you," he told her. Then looking up nervously, added, "You're different then my other grandma. She smells like chocolate chip cookies and likes to play Go Fish. Do you like Go Fish?"

Both Lexie and Grayson inhaled, neither expecting the turn in the conversation. It was obvious by the slow drain of color on his mother's face that she was not only confused, but extremely uncomfortable. "Go what?" she asked, reacting as if Ryan had just sworn at her.

Ryan stepped back and clung to Lexie's leg. Grayson reached over and patted his shoulder, smiling at him in reassurance.

"Grayson, what does he mean?" Her voice cracked, and her jaw opened and closed multiple times with no further sound. She ran her long fingers over her neck, almost as if attempting to dislodge an imaginative item stuck in her throat. She swallowed, and spoke in a broken voice. "What is this? Who are these people?"

Lexie pulled Ryan tighter against her side, struggling to keep silent as Grayson's mother's tone all but spit on them as unworthy of her.

"Grayson, I'm going to take Ryan to see the horses," Lexie said, her tone sharp.

His mother stood up straight, and whipped her head around

to stare at Grayson incredulously. "You aren't seriously going to let them wander the grounds alone are you? I don't think that is a wise idea at all." She turned to Lexie and eyed her suspiciously.

Grayson stepped in between them, attempting to break their stare down. "It'll be fine, Mother. Besides, you and I need to talk."

His mother looked around him and locked eyes with Lexie. She was shocked by the venom in the older woman's eyes.

"That's a good idea," Lexie said to Grayson. "You go speak to your mother, and come find us after you've located and hidden all of the sharp objects."

Grayson chuckled and then cleared his throat to cover up the sound. Lexie smiled at his mother, a sarcastic syrupy smile, and was pleased to see her eyes grow wide, and her mouth drop open in shock.

Chapter 34

Grayson followed the path that led from the house to the barns. Hearing the whinny of the horses and the commands of the trainers in the breaking pens brought a smile to his face. He'd missed this—the smells, the openness, the activity…all of it. He'd grown up with reins in his hands and the expectation of taking over the family business. His father had understood his need to break away, to take his own path, but his mother was another story. She was used to having things her way and her only child becoming a soldier, then a police officer, was not in her plan. Neither was becoming a grandmother to a four-year-old.

He took a deep breath and tried to remind himself she was in shock. Her reaction had been less than gracious, even bordering on snobbish and rude. The fact that he'd asked his mother if she'd known all along and chosen to keep it from him hadn't helped his cause. He was sure she hadn't known, but it didn't make sense. Maggie heard he'd died from somewhere, but where? Who would have told her such a lie? It was obviously someone she believed would know. But if it had been a member of his family, it wouldn't be like Maggie to keep Ryan a secret. Would it?

Maggie and his mother had never gotten along. If he were to be honest with himself, very few people got along with his mother. She was opinionated, aloof, and had the ability to be as cold as Alaska in January. She had never approved of Maggie, thought she was beneath him, and after ranting about Lexie for ten minutes, he'd learned his mother thought even less of her than she had Maggie.

He smiled, recalling the scene between his mother and Lexie on the porch earlier. Lexie had stood up to his mother in her typical way; sarcasm served with a warm smile. No, the two of them would not be friends anytime soon. He supposed it didn't matter at this point. Lexie would be Ryan's mother, and he hoped they could be friends, but he knew they couldn't be anything more. Even in the knowing, the pain was undeniable.

He spotted her leaning against the fence of one of the breaking pens, pointing at the horse and trainer while talking to Ryan. Ryan stood on the bottom rung of the fence, his mouth parted, and his eyes wide with awe. He tried to focus on the warm feeling flowing over him as he watched his son, mesmerized by the beauty in front of him, instead of the way Lexie's jeans stretched across her hips. It seemed unfair to still want her the way he did.

Having heard his footsteps, they both turned around. Ryan's face broke into a huge grin. "Mom says maybe you'll take me riding," he said pulling Grayson's hand. "Can we go now?"

Grayson smiled at Ryan's excitement and looked over at Lexie. The wind tossed her hair, blowing it softly across her cheeks and carrying the faint scent of her perfume toward him. The setting sun shone from behind her creating a halo of light. She still took his breath away.

Closing his eyes and shaking his head, he turned to Ryan before opening them again. "We have to be in for dinner soon, but how about we take a ride first thing in the morning?"

Ryan jumped up and down with excitement. "Yes!" He shouted. "I want that horse." He pointed to the sixteen-hand chestnut colored thoroughbred rearing up on his hind legs in the middle of the round pen.

"I think we might need to start off on a different horse for now," he said, patting Ryan on the shoulder trying to keep the laughter out of his voice. "Maybe one that's not so high strung for your first ride."

"Okay, but I want a big one," Ryan added, taking his hand and walking with him toward the house.

Grayson looked over at Lexie. "You're welcome to join us," he told her. "Could be a lot of fun."

She nodded her head and attempted to smile, but didn't speak as she followed beside them.

"Dinner is a bit of a formal affair, I'm sorry to say," Grayson told her. "My mother tends to overdo it normally, so you can imagine the scene when we have guests."

"With your mother's warmth and graciousness, I'm sure her table is surrounded by guests regularly," Lexie said sarcastically.

Grayson chuckled. "Yeah, she definitely has a way about her."

Lexie grunted, and then sighed. "Grayson, I don't have anything dressy packed. I thought this was a ranch, remember?"

"I'm sure anything you brought will be fine. You always look beautiful." Grayson realized he'd spoken out loud when Lexie looked at him with confusion. You need a muzzle, he thought to himself. Choosing to pretend he'd never said it, he bent down to Ryan. "Why don't you run ahead and have Annie show you your room. We're right behind you." As soon as Ryan pulled far enough ahead, he stopped and turned to Lexie. "I'm sorry about my mother's behavior earlier. She's still not happy I'm living in California, and once she spotted you, I think she may have believed you were part of the reason I stayed there."

"I don't think she would have behaved much differently if I lived next door, Grayson." She shook her head, and smiled at him. He got the impression she was silently telling him he was a moron.

"She can be a bit judgmental, but she'll come around." Grayson said, unsure if he was trying to convince her or himself. "She has to, for Ryan's sake."

"How did that go by the way?" Lexie asked as they made their way toward the house.

"I don't think it's real for her yet. Hell, I'm not sure it's real for me yet."

Chapter 35

Fresh from a shower and standing in a fluffy pink towel, Lexie was becoming frustrated as she pulled clothes from her suitcase. She threw a pair of jeans onto the stack piling up on the bed. Who threw a formal dinner on a Thursday night? She'd believed they were staying on a ranch, and packed accordingly. This wasn't like any ranch she'd ever seen. Judging by the outfit his mother had worn at four in the afternoon, dinner would be tuxedos and evening gowns.

Finally settling on the only pair of slacks she'd brought and a simple sweater, she'd just turned toward the bathroom when there was a knock on the door. Throwing a robe over her towel, she opened the door, surprised to see Darla Mae on the other side.

Smiling sweetly, Darla Mae asked, "May I come in?"

Lexie held the door open and let her enter. "What can I do for you?" She asked smartly, not buying her nice girl act for a minute.

"Grayson mentioned you might not have packed the appropriate dinner attire. I thought I might be able to help." Darla Mae laid a red dress across the bed.

Stammering, Lexie tried to speak. "That's very nice of you, but I did pack a pair of slacks I was going to wear."

Darla Mae looked at her sympathetically. "It's your choice, of course, but I would recommend you take me up on my offer. Lydia Hunter likes things her way. I'd hate to see your second impression play out as badly as your first."

With those words, Darla Mae turned and walked out of the bedroom, leaving the dress on the bed and silently closing the door behind her.

Lexie looked down at the dress. It seemed innocent enough. So why did she get the feeling it wasn't? She supposed it could be laced with itching powder, or previously worn by a dead relative causing Mrs. Hunter to break out into hysterics. She shook her head and laughed at herself.

"What's funny, Mom?" Ryan asked, walking into the room tugging on his shirt collar.

Kneeling down, she told him it was nothing as she tucked his shirt into the back of the khaki pants she'd packed for him, and straightened his hair.

"Grayson told me to tell you dinner's in fifteen minutes." He said, plopping on the bed. "Why do I have to wear this just to eat dinner?" He tugged on his collar again.

"Mrs. Hunter wanted to have a fancy dinner to welcome us to her home," Lexie explained, heading for the mirror to put on her make-up.

Ryan grunted and continued to pull on his collar.

Lexie slipped into the dress, surprised at how well it fit her. It was sleeveless and tied around the waist, falling just below her knees with a small gathering of red feathers at the hem. She pulled on the simple black pumps she'd brought, and stood studying her reflection in the mirror. She looked good, and she wasn't itching, so far so good, she thought. Taking Ryan's hand, they headed down the stairs to the dining room.

A tall, older man in a black suit and white gloves nodded his head in greeting to them and waved them toward the two empty seats on either side of Lydia Hunter. That she hadn't burst into tears when she saw the dress was another good sign. Lexie allowed herself to relax, and sipped on a glass of champagne that had been placed in front of her.

Grayson was sitting beside Ryan and Darla Mae beside her. He smiled broadly when a taller, somewhat older version of him walked into the dining room. Standing at the end of the table, Grayson's father smiled warmly at his son, his happiness to see him shone through his eyes. Grayson stood up from the table and embraced him.

With his arm around his father, the two of them walked toward Ryan. "Dad, this is my son, Ryan. Ryan, this is your grandfather, William Hunter."

With wonder in his eyes, William Hunter bent down and took Ryan's hand. "It's very nice to meet you," he said, shaking his hand. "I understand you like the horses and would like to go for a ride."

Ryan nodded his head hard enough to lose his balance on the chair. William laughed, a wonderful baritone sound, and steadied Ryan on his chair.

"I would love it if you would go riding with me tomorrow." William looked over at Lexie with warm, yet observant eyes. "That is, if it's okay with your mom."

"Can I, Mom? Please?" Ryan begged.

"I think he would enjoy that," she replied to William. Then turning to her son, she added, "But you have to promise to do exactly as William tells you. Best behavior, deal?"

Ryan's eyes lit up, and he nodded his head again. "Oh, thank you, William, thank you. I promise to be good."

"If you're okay with it, I'd very much like it if you called me Grandfather." William's eyes were misty as he took his place at the head of the table.

Lexie glanced over at Lydia and wasn't surprised to see the disapproval in her eyes. She wasn't going to accept Ryan until she had hard evidence, that much was clear.

The servers placed bowls of spicy pumpkin soup in front of each of them. The aroma made her mouth water, and it wasn't until then that she realized she hadn't eaten anything but airplane peanuts all day. She reached for her spoon and paused. Everyone was sitting quietly with their hands in their laps. Ryan lifted his spoon and stirred it around his soup bowl, causing it to slosh from the bowl and onto the charger beneath. Noticing the disapproval on Lydia's face, she reached over and placed her hand over his to still his spoon.

"Why is nobody eating?" Ryan whispered loudly. "Do they not like it either?"

William reached for his spoon and winked at Ryan. "It's delicious, give it a try," he coaxed.

She realized that everyone had been waiting for William to begin eating first. Strange ritual, she thought, but one she would be sure to remember during her stay.

Ryan took a spoonful of the soup and scrunched his face, swallowing it loudly. "Mom, this is gross, do I have to eat it?"

"Ryan, you're being rude," she scolded quietly into his ear. "The proper thing is to eat part of it—without complaining."

"But it tastes like hot punkin pie," he replied, again in a very loud whisper. "I don't like punkin pie. It's gross."

"I didn't like pumpkin pie when I was a boy either," William said pushing his bowl from him. "I think you and I should wait for the next course. You like pork chops, I hope."

Ryan beamed with relief. "I love 'em," he replied.

Lexie smiled thankfully at William, and lifted her spoon. The soup was wonderful, and she finished every drop. She wanted to lift the bowl and lick it clean, and would have loved to see Lydia's face if she had.

Feeling eyes on her, Lexie looked over at Lydia, and caught the disapproving glare. Now what, she thought, remaining silent.

"Your dress is an interesting color. Do you wear a lot of red?" Lydia asked, her nose wrinkled with disapproval.

"Pardon me?" Lexie asked, uncomfortable with the look on her face.

"Do you wear a lot of red?" Lydia repeated.

Lexie looked down at herself. Interesting color? It was red, a simple shade of red. Looking back up, she studied Lydia, and tried to understand exactly what she was getting at. "I wear it occasionally."

"Well, I suppose it would be just a color to you," Lydia said arrogantly. "My people tend to shy away from colors that are meant for brothels and street corners."

Heat rose up Lexie's face, and she glared across the table at Darla Mae. Now she understood why she'd been so helpful with her wardrobe. She whipped her head around to give Lydia a piece of her mind, but before she could get the words out, Grayson stood up and curtly asked his mother if they could speak in the kitchen.

Lydia smiled innocently at him, and quietly followed him from the dining room.

"Lexie, please accept my apologies on my wife's behalf. I don't know what has gotten into her. I'm sure she didn't mean it the way it sounded," William said, trying to calm the situation.

She smiled at him and lifted her glass. "She meant exactly what she said," she muttered to herself.

When Grayson and Lydia returned to the dining room, he mouthed he was sorry and sat quietly waiting.

"Mother," he prompted, "don't you have something you would like to say?"

Looking as if she was attempting to speak with a mouth full of broken glass, she said, "Lexie, I apologize for my choice of words."

Smiling sweetly, Lexie replied, "No, you're right. I should have realized this was a dress best suited for a paid professional the moment I borrowed it from Darla Mae."

Lexie hid her smile by taking another sip of her champagne, as both Darla Mae and Lydia gasped in shock.

Chapter 36

Grayson found Lexie swaying in a tall white rocking chair on the side of the house. The sun was setting behind the trees on the other side of the pasture, shooting bright orange streaks across the sky.

"It's beautiful here this time of night," he said, sitting down in the empty chair beside her.

She nodded, and continued to rock, staring straight ahead. He watched her, studying her profile in the dim light. Her long eyelashes fluttered softly, and her lips pursed out in a thoughtful pout. Small wisps of her dark hair blew across her cheeks, caressing her skin. Desperate to reach out and stroke her cheeks, or to kiss the tenseness from her lips, he forced himself to sit back in the chair and look away from her.

"I can't apologize enough for my mother's behavior today." He said in a genuine tone. "I don't understand her, so I can't even begin to explain the why's to you."

"She doesn't like me. I'm okay with that. I'm not too fond of her either, if we're going to be honest," Lexie told him.

"I don't think she's ever met anyone like you," he said chuckling. "I don't think there's been a time in her life where someone's spoken back to her."

She turned and looked at him. "She doesn't want to believe Ryan is your son. Are you planning on taking him in for a blood test? He's scared to death of needles, you know."

"Not now." Grayson kicked his feet up on the railing of the porch. "It may come down to that for legal purposes, but I know he's my son, and that's all that really matters."

"What legal purposes?" She asked, her voice laden with fear.

Turning to look at her, he was surprised by the anxiety on her face. "I was referring to Ryan's legal right to inherit all of this someday." Grayson waited for her to meet his eyes before asking,

"Do you honestly still believe that I would take Ryan from you?"

Looking away from him, she didn't answer.

The pain in her silence was excruciating. How could she believe him capable of destroying their family? Maggie may have given birth to Ryan, but Lexie was his mother. And sadly, she didn't have the slightest bit of faith in him.

Breaking the silence, Lexie's voice was venomous when she asked, "Is that her problem, that he would be next in line for the Hunter throne?"

Grayson sighed loudly, struggling to calm his anger. He wanted to shake her, scream and yell, make her realize the damage she was causing by having lost faith in him, by letting her fears and insecurities cloud her judgment. This was not about his mother or her inability to accept that he had a son, this was about Lexie, and her inability to believe he only wanted what was best for Ryan; and her too, if he were to be honest. Everything he'd ever dreamt of had been right at his fingertips, and in one crushing blow, Lexie had scattered them to the winds.

"Grayson?"

He turned to look at her, realizing she'd been waiting for his answer. He stood up, sadly shaking his head. "Good night, Lexie. I'll check on Ryan before I turn in."

Without waiting for her to reply, he walked away, leaving her alone on the porch.

*

Lexie wiped the tear from her cheek, pulled her knees to her chest and rested her forehead against them. She was such an idiot. Why couldn't she just believe Grayson when he told her he had no intentions of taking Ryan away? Why did she still wonder if he'd known about Maggie's pregnancy and chose to ignore it?

Everything she'd learned about him, told her he wasn't capable of such cruelty, but still she questioned him. She hoped it was due to the truth that things weren't adding up, and not because she was incapable of trusting him.

She jumped, startled by the sound of an angry voice cutting through the silence. The voice was Darla Mae's. Curious, she tiptoed down the steps onto the grass and slowly made her way toward her.

Darla Mae had her back to Lexie and was speaking into her cell phone. "I don't know how he found out," she snapped. "I just know he knows." She ran her hand through her hair in obvious frustration.

Stepping behind a tree to avoid being seen, Lexie wondered who the "he" was.

"I don't know." Darla Mae paused. "I know that, I'm not an idiot." There was another pause as she listened to the person on the other end of the phone. "How is *this* my fault?"

An owl howled above her, causing her to squeak in surprise. Darla Mae whipped around but Lexie managed to flatten herself against the large tree and remain undetected.

"It's William we need to worry about. He's as happy as a pig in mud."

Lexie wished she could hear the other side of the conversation. Something about this made her uneasy, a gut reaction she couldn't identify.

"I'm trying. What do you want me to do that I haven't already tried?"

The back door opened emitting a path of light across the lawn. "Mommy?" she heard Ryan call out. "Are you out here?"

"I've got to go, the brat has the door hanging wide open and I don't need anyone to see me outside in the dark on the damn phone."

Lexie held her breath.

Darla Mae's voice softened, "Ryan, honey, your mom's not out here, it's just me. Go on back inside now."

The door closed and Darla Mae's voice hardened. "Yes, I know. Don't I always?"

Lexie heard the phone snap closed and watched Darla Mae walk in through the back door. She waited a few minutes before she rounded the house by the porch and let herself inside.

Chapter 37

The air was still crisp, but the sun was already drying the dew from the grass outside the barn. Ryan was bouncing with unconcealed excitement as Grayson saddled the horse they'd be riding.

"Can we go fast?" He asked, tugging on Grayson's sleeve.

"We have to start slow, but we can work up to fast." Grayson answered, sliding the bit into Abby's mouth and securing the bridle behind her ears.

William laughed from up in his saddle. "You're a natural horseman, Ryan. You'll be racing over these hills in no time."

"Ready?" Grayson asked.

Ryan nodded, standing in awe as he looked from the horse to Grayson.

"Abby's a good girl, she won't hurt you. Don't worry," Grayson said, waving to the stable hand that walked over with a step stool.

Once Ryan was settled in his saddle and his stirrups were adjusted, his face beamed with joy. He leaned forward, rubbing and patting Abby's neck. Grayson took hold of the reins, slowly leading them in a large circle in front of the barn, making sure Ryan knew the feel of the horse beneath him. He explained the use of the reins, and that Abby would know to follow along with their horses.

Ryan's face was locked in serious concentration, his eyes taking in every move Grayson showed him. Grayson had to admit, he seemed like a natural horseman, just like William said.

Stopping them beside his father, Grayson handed the reins to Ryan, showing him how to hold them. He climbed onto the back of the horse and let Ryan lead as the three of them slowly made their way around the barn, and down the trail that cut through the pastures.

Ryan sat with his back straight, and his eyes wide with wonder. He turned and grinned at both of them. "Grayson, do you think we could live here instead of California? I want to be a cowboy instead of a cop."

Grayson laughed, "I, however, am a cop in California, and your mom has her shop there. How about if we just make sure to visit often and work on your cowboy skills when we do?"

"How come the cowboy's don't wear hats and buckles and stuff?" Ryan asked.

"Ours is a bit different than a normal ranch." William explained. "Here we raise and train race horses. We have jockeys instead of cowboys. But some of the workers still wear hats and buckles and stuff."

Ryan shrugged his shoulders, "I think the cowboys are cooler."

"You know what I think?" William added. "I think this young man is right and he needs a trip into town for some proper cowboy attire."

"Do you mean like a cowboy hat and pointy boots?" Ryan asked with wide eyes.

"Exactly what I mean," William clarified.

"Cool," Ryan said, and turned his focus back to the trail in front of them.

When they reached the river that flowed through the back acres, they decided to stop and rest. The moment he'd dismounted Ryan raced to the rocks that jetted out across the water.

Sitting in the grass beside his father, Grayson shouted, "Be careful Ryan, those rocks can be slippery." He laughed when his son turned and waved his hand dismissing the warning. Ryan was fearless, just like he'd been at his age.

William turned to Grayson. "I'm sorry about your mother's behavior. I don't understand what's gotten into her lately."

Grayson remained silent for a moment, trying to find the right way to word the question he really wanted to ask. "Dad, you didn't know Maggie was pregnant did you?"

"How can you even ask that question?" His father asked, his eyes filled with hurt.

"You're right, I apologize." Grayson picked a piece of grass and busied his hands tying it into knots. "It's just that none of this makes sense. Maggie believed I was dead, but where would she have gotten that idea? And when she got sick, why didn't she come to you and Mother?"

"You're going to have to catch me up. I still don't know most of the story."

Crossing his feet at the ankles and leaning back on his elbows, careful to keep Ryan in his sights, Grayson filled his father in on meeting Lexie, Maggie's journals, and his disappointment in Lexie's reaction to the discovery.

"You love this girl, don't you?" His father asked.

"It wouldn't matter if I did; it can never work out between us." Grayson said, averting his gaze.

"Never say never, son. And for what it's worth, I like her. She's got spunk." His father chuckled. "I can't tell you how much I enjoyed dinner last night. I know your mother behaved horribly, but the retort from Lexie and your mother's subsequent speechlessness was priceless."

"She definitely has a way with words." Grayson said, smiling at the memory.

"She's a good mother, too. Something you need to think about," his father added. "I just think it would be a shame for you to become an every-other-weekend parent when you've already missed so much time with him."

"I won't be an every-other-weekend father. That's not even an option." Grayson replied, his tone sharp. "I don't want to talk about Lexie right now," he said, taking a deep breath. "Ryan, that's far enough," he shouted. Turning back to his father, he said, "Can you think of who could have given Maggie the idea that I'd died in Iraq? I can't think of anyone, and it would have to have been someone she would believe."

"You're asking me if I think your mother is capable of such a thing," his father locked eyes with him. "I just can't believe she is. I know she never approved of Maggie, and she all but threatened to kill herself if you married her, but to tell her you were dead…I think that's even out of her realm of acceptable meddling."

"Who could have told her something like that, lied to her like that?" Grayson shook his head. "I just can't fathom where this information came from."

His father reached over and patted him on the shoulder. "I can only imagine how frustrating it must be not to know, but in all honesty, does it really matter now?"

Grayson clenched his jaw. "It does if that person lied to her knowing she was pregnant with my son."

Chapter 38

"Jordan, I need a favor."

"Of course you do, Lex," her brother chuckled into the other end of the phone. "Let me guess, bail money?"

"Very funny," she replied. "I'm serious."

"So am I," Jordan told her. "You've been with Darla Mae for over forty-eight hours now. I'm surprised it took you this long before you physically assaulted her."

"Trust me when I tell you I'm amazed by own self-control." She smiled to herself imagining Darla Mae's throat clenched in her hands. "But it is about Darla Mae."

"Of course it is."

"I overheard her on the phone last night, and something isn't right." She stood up and walked to the window of her room, looking out over the green pastures that stretched as far as she could see. "I want you to run a background check on her. I know it's asking a lot, but I'm serious. She's up to something."

"Okay," he said, surprising her with his lack of questions. "I need her full name and date of birth."

Lexie had snuck into Darla Mae's purse last night and written down the information. She pulled the piece of paper from the pocket of her jeans and read it to him.

"I'll see what I can find."

"Thanks, Jordan, I mean that," she told him.

"No problem. How are things?" He asked. "Have you and Grayson kissed and made up yet?"

"No, there will be no making up. I've pretty much ruined this one for myself." She watched as two horses and their riders made their way down a path running between the white fences of the pastures. Tears filled her eyes as she watched her son, sitting tall and proud on top of the horse, with Grayson riding behind him. "He will never forgive me for doubting him."

"Give him time, Lex," Jordan said reassuringly. "It's got to be a lot for him to take in, learning he is a father would be enough of an adjustment. But to know that the woman he fell in love with questioned his values as a man has got to be a difficult pill to swallow. He'll come around."

"I appreciate your optimism, but I don't think so. I hurt him too deeply. I think in time he'll forgive me, but he'll never let me in again." She wiped a tear from her cheek as she watched Grayson lift her son from the horse and spin him around before setting him down.

Saying her goodbyes to her brother, she hung up and headed downstairs to meet Ryan.

A few minutes later, Ryan came bursting through the door, his face flushed with excitement. "Mom, you shoulda seen me. I was leading the way. Grayson let me lead through the trail, and now I get to go get a real cowboy hat and pointy boots 'cause I'm a real cowboy now."

She smiled at his breathless replay of his morning ride. "Grandfather said I'm a natural. I don't know exactly what that is, but I think it means I'm a real cowboy now. Grayson says we can't live here, but I can come visit and learn more cowboy stuff a lot. Isn't that cool?"

"Very cool," she told him, helping him out of his dirty tennis shoes.

She smiled at Grayson and William as they walked in. "I hear we have a cowboy in our midst, and *Grandfather* said he was a natural."

William's eyes welled with tears of pride. "He is a natural. He's a Hunter after all."

An irritated voice spoke up from behind them, startling them all. "William, may I speak to you a moment. Alone."

When Lexie turned around, she saw Lydia in the hallway, her hand on her jutted hip, her mouth was a straight line, and her eyes blazed with fury. She turned to look at William, and saw a flash of irritation before he excused himself and followed Lydia down the hallway and into the den.

"Ryan, head upstairs, change your clothes and wash your hands while I get you some lunch," Lexie told her son, before turning back to Grayson. "Why is your mother upset with William?"

"If I know my mother, it's a combination of his excitement at being called grandfather, and his referring to Ryan as a Hunter." Grayson stared at the closed door of the den and added, "I don't know how he's put up with her for forty years."

Lexie looked at him sympathetically. "Are you okay? It can't be easy for you that she is struggling to accept your son."

"No, it's not easy." He sighed. "But it's expected. She has a love for money that's never been reduced by family. Her priorities are green. Always were."

"I'm sorry for that," Lexie said honestly.

Grayson smiled faintly and reached over to squeeze her hand. "Thanks, but I'm used to it. I'll go check on Ryan. Don't worry about making lunch, Lila will already have that handled."

She watched him walk away, her heart breaking for him. It was one thing to know his mother didn't approve of her, but another altogether to see that way she was hurting him. She'd be damned if she let that woman ever hurt her son in that way.

Her cell phone rang in the pocket of her sweater, and she stepped out the back door when she saw it was Jordan.

"That was fast," she told him when she answered.

"I'm amazing, it's okay, you can say it," he teased.

"What'd you find?" she asked anxiously.

"Not a lot. No criminal record, no marriages or births. Most of the information I was able to obtain was in reference to her family." He told her. "Her father had been married previously to a woman named Charlotte Adkins. They had a son, but there is no record of him or Charlotte after the divorce. No child support payments, no filed visitation schedule, nothing. It's like they both just disappeared."

"She has a half-brother?" Lexie asked, surprised.

"Looks that way," Jordan answered. "Her parents married shortly after his divorce and she was born eight months later. Darla Mae's father inherited a large ranch when he was in his early twenties, and made it a huge success raising thoroughbreds, a bit like Grayson's family. But there were some financial troubles. Mr. Pruitt was a huge gambler, and not very good at it from the looks of things." She could hear Jordan shuffling through papers before he continued. "He basically lost everything betting on a horse race. Interestingly enough, it was one of the Hunter's prized horses that beat his, and all but bankrupted him."

"That is interesting," she said. "They must have had some bad blood between them after that."

"I suppose there would've been, but Pruitt and his wife died within three weeks of the race. Pruitt drove through a barrier and went over a cliff on the hills, only two miles from their home. His wife was in the car with him."

"That couldn't have been easy for Darla Mae," she said, uncomfortable with the flash of pity she was feeling.

"I couldn't imagine losing both our parents, let alone at once," Jordan stated, agreeing with her. "The Hunters purchased some of the better horses from the Pruitt's estate, and assisted with finding a buyer for the ranch to pay off Mr. Pruitt's debt. They filed for guardianship of Darla Mae, and the rest, as they say, is history."

"I wonder why they took her in," she questioned. "Do you think it was misplaced guilt, or were they close enough to the Pruitt's to have a genuine bond with Darla Mae?"

"It doesn't appear that they were close. There was a lawsuit involving the alleged drugging of the Pruitt's racehorses, filed by the Hunters."

"They accused the Pruitt's of using enhancement drugs?" She asked.

"Looks that way. The other thing that's a bit strange is the car accident itself. Originally, there were questions about whether or not it was an accident, or suicide, but before anything was determined, it seems to just go away. It was listed as an accident, and there is no record of a thorough investigation."

"How is that possible?"

"In my experience, that normally means one thing. Somebody with enough clout was able to brush it under the rug and let it die where it was." Jordan explained.

"Or someone with enough money to buy the rug they brushed it under." Lexie said, struggling to put the pieces together in her head.

"Money can do a lot of things. As much as it pisses me off, that includes covering up things people don't want discovered."

"Thanks, Jordan, for looking into this for me."

"I wish I knew what you were looking for," he told her honestly. "What any of this has to do with cryptic phone conversations I can't guess."

"I don't know, but I promise you, I will find out."

Chapter 39

With her feet tucked up beside her, Lexie sat on a bench swing in the corner of the massive yard, watching the horses graze on the rich green grass in the pasture. She continued to go over her conversation with Jordan, moving the pieces around mentally, and finding it no less confusing.

If Darla Mae had a half-brother, were they in contact with each other? Did she know he existed? She would have to assume Darla Mae would know. If her father had previously been married, it wouldn't be a huge shock. At least she wouldn't think so.

"Can I join you?"

Lexie jumped, startled when she realized she was no longer alone. "Of course, sorry Mr. Hunter, I didn't see you."

William Hunter sat down in the swing beside her. "That's because your mind was a million miles away. And please, call me William."

Lexie smiled at him. The more she got to know William, the more and more surprised she was by his relationship with his wife. They were so different. Lydia was negative, judgmental, controlling, and rude. William was kind, loving, always spoke positively, and smiled easily. He was also a saint, she thought, cringing at the thought of her last confrontation with Lydia.

"How are you holding up?" William asked her, giving the swing a push. "These recent events must be a lot for you take in."

She slowly nodded her head. "It certainly has. How many women can say that they discovered they were dating their son's dead father?" She chuckled, sarcastically. "I still can't believe I can say it."

"Grayson mentioned something about that," William continued. "Why did Margaret believe Grayson was dead? I'm struggling to understand it."

Lexie sat back in the swing. "That's what I'm trying to figure out, because it doesn't make sense." She looked at William pensively.

"When did you last see Maggie?" She'd never called her Margaret, and couldn't see that changing now.

"I'd only met her once." William's eyes grew distant as he seemed to go back in time. "Grayson was in love and couldn't wait to bring her home. At least that's how I saw it. He showed up with her two weeks after meeting her in New York and announced she was returning to the post with him. Needless to say, Lydia was far from thrilled."

Lexie grunted, causing William to laugh.

"She's a tough one, my Lydia. I don't think she'll ever consider anyone good enough for our son." He turned and looked at her. His eyes were the same smoky blue as Grayson, and she felt as if he were looking straight into her heart with the piercing knowledge she saw there. "But Grayson is smart enough to know when a woman is good enough for him." He stated. "You know Margaret was good for him, and more importantly, you know you are as well."

She bent her head down, willing the tears not to fall and give her away. "I never knew them together, obviously, but I knew Maggie, and any man would have been lucky to be loved by her. She loved Grayson very much."

"And you?" He asked.

She lifted her chin to look at him. The understanding she saw in his eyes crumbled the last of her will, and warm tears rolled down her cheeks. She opened her mouth to speak, but couldn't get the words past the lump in her throat. William reached into his pocket and pulled out a monogramed handkerchief. Handing it to her, he silently watched her, waiting.

"I did…I do," she mumbled. "But I blew it. I committed the ultimate sin as far as Grayson is concerned." She met his eyes. "I didn't believe in him." She wiped her eyes as another flow of tears began. "I questioned his motives, and even worse, his true feelings for not only myself, but Maggie, and Ryan as well."

"Is that unforgiveable?" he asked her seriously.

She nodded her head. "He'll never see me in the same way again."

"Never say never, Alexis." He smiled at her.

She laughed nervously. "How did we get onto this subject?"

"You were asking me about Margaret."

"Oh yeah, that's right," she folded the handkerchief on her lap. "You only met her once, you said. She never called you again, after Grayson was deployed?"

"No, she didn't. That's the baffling part. Lydia was about as warm and welcoming to Margaret as she was to you, but she and I were different. There was a spark in her. It wasn't quite as bright and vocal as yours," he laughed aloud. "But it was there. She'd lost her parents early on, and said I'd be the one she'd choose if she could pick an earthly replacement father. That girl had me wrapped around her little finger almost as tightly as she had my son." He smiled at the memory.

"She was a wonderful woman," Lexie agreed.

"She knew I cared for her. I called her right after I received my first call from Grayson in Iraq and he told me that she'd left him. It didn't make sense to me. I knew she loved him. In fact, I called multiple times. The first couple I always got her voicemail but she never called back. The last time I called, the number had been disconnected."

"She never told you she was pregnant?"

This time it was William's eyes that welled with tears. "She didn't. I honestly can't understand why."

"Did Grayson tell you why she broke off the relationship? That she was sick?" Lexie asked.

"He did." William reached over and squeezed her hand. "I'm sorry for your loss as well."

She nodded her head.

"You were with her?" He asked. "When she passed?"

"I was, yes." She told him, remembering the day as if it were only yesterday. "She was holding Ryan. She loved that little boy."

"And so do you."

"Very much," she said.

They both sat in silence for a while, watching the horses graze, and the wind blow through the trees, causing them to dance and sway.

"Grayson tells me you're a volunteer at Nathan's Hope." William said. "That can't be easy after your time with Maggie."

"Nothing about cancer is easy," she told him, "but I love that I can help, even in a small way."

"And you are friends with Aimee Morrison? Or should I say, Aimee Lee now?" He asked.

"Yes, I am. I met Aimee when she was working as Emily's assistant and I volunteered at the Charity Auction. She's an amazing woman. I couldn't be happier for both her and Emily, being reunited after all those years."

"I made a trip out there the following year for the auction and couldn't believe how happy Emily was. I don't know if I've ever seen anyone that radiant before." William threw one leg over his knee and leaned back in the swing.

"You should have seen her at the wedding. She was breathtaking, even when she cried." Lexie grinned.

"I take it you've heard the news about the engagement."

Lexie's eyes grew wide. "What engagement?"

"I've just received an announcement that Emily Sinclair will be marrying Robert Lund next spring."

"What?" Lexie's mouth dropped open. Closing it again, a grin spread across her face. "I knew it! I'm so happy for her." Her eyes grew serious again and she spoke aloud, but to herself. "I wonder why I didn't receive an announcement or why Aimee didn't call me. She must be so excited that her Uncle Bob and her Mother found each other."

"Maybe you did receive one, but you're not home to get it, and I'm sure Aimee knows that you're a bit distracted right now." William patted her on the knee in a fatherly calming fashion.

She smiled at him and nodded her head. "You're probably right."

He stood up from the swing and turned to her. "It's nice to witness someone finding love a second time in their life when they never thought they'd survive the loss of the first one." He winked at her and walked back toward the house.

Somehow she didn't think he was talking about Emily Sinclair.

Chapter 40

After sending Ryan with Billy, the family's long time barn foreman, to help with the evening feeding, he went in search of Lexie. He hadn't seen her since returning from their ride this morning, and he wanted to make sure his mother hadn't had her kidnapped and shipped off to Timbuktu. He laughed to himself as he pictured that scene. He should have known Lexie wouldn't sit back quietly and let his mother walk over her. He couldn't remember a time when his mother had been left speechless before this week.

He spotted her walking toward the creek, and hurried his steps to catch up to her. Reaching her side, he interrupted an apparently deep conversation she was having with herself.

"Where have you been all day?" he asked her. "Just walking around talking to yourself?"

She smiled sarcastically and replied, "No, actually, I spoke to a couple of the horses, bonded with a very inquisitive squirrel, and even found time to talk to your father."

"Wow, you've been chatty," he laughed. "Mind if I tag along on your walk?"

"No, I'd like that," she said, her heart rate increasing just being beside him. "Where's Ryan?"

"He's helping Billy feed the horses. That boy is crazy about horses. I hope Little League will be enough when we get home." He chuckled.

"He seems to be having a great time, and your father is so good with him," she said, stepping over a low rock wall and cutting across toward the river.

"My father's a good man. I think he's pretty happy that he's a grandfather, even if it was a bit of a shock." He held out his hand to her and helped her step down from one of the large rocks along the riverbank.

"I think so too." She smiled at him and sat down on one of the flatter boulders. "He seemed genuinely shocked that Maggie didn't contact him about the baby."

Grayson plopped down onto the rock beside her, stunned that his father would tell her that. "When did you speak to my father about Maggie?"

"Earlier today," she answered, her brow creased with confusion. "Are you upset that we spoke, or upset that we spoke about Maggie?" she snapped.

He studied her for a moment before replying. Realizing she was defensive, he answered carefully. "I don't have any problem with you talking to my father, and certainly no issues with you discussing Maggie, I was just surprised."

She picked up a small rock and tossed it into the water. "I'm just trying to figure out what happened. I need to know why Maggie died thinking Ryan would be alone, and why she never told your family. I also can't understand why she never mentioned your family to me. Not to mention she thought you were dead. Somebody knows something around here."

"You're not the only one with unanswered questions, Lexie." His voice rose, anger boiling beneath the surface.

Her eyes fluttered down. "That's not what I meant...I just..."

"You just what, Lexie? You believe there is some big conspiracy to keep me separated from my son? That someone maliciously kept the truth from me?" His voice was venomous.

Looking at the surprise in her eyes, he stood up, ashamed at himself for taking his frustration out on her. He knew deep down he wondered the same thing, and worse, wondered if it could be someone in his own family.

"I'm sorry, Lexie. I didn't mean to yell at you." He kicked at a loose rock beneath his boot. "I don't have the slightest idea how to figure this out, what questions to ask and of whom."

She didn't respond and continued to intently study the long

blade of grass she'd picked out of the cracks between the rocks. He turned to leave, but stopped at the quiet question she asked him.

"Were you angry enough with Maggie to knowingly let her believe you were dead?"

Grayson took a moment to control the sudden surge of pain that shot through him, afraid it would release itself in an angry response. He turned to look at her, and was surprised by the pain he saw resonating in her eyes. "No," he answered her honestly, "I wasn't. I loved her and no matter how much she'd hurt me, I could never do something like that."

"I think I knew that," she told him, before turning her head away. "I'm sorry I felt I had to ask. You didn't deserve that."

"No, I didn't," he said and waited for her to look at him. "But for what it's worth, I get it. She was your friend."

Tears rolled down Lexie's face stopping his retreat. "I miss her."

He sat back down beside her and putting his arm around her shoulder, pulled her to his side, and let her cry on his shoulder. The breeze carried her scent and the heat from her body seeped into him, hitting him like a fist punch to his gut. He wasn't convinced he'd ever be able to get her out of his system, and worse, his heart.

Sitting up, she wiped her face, and smiled weakly. "Sorry about that. You have mascara all over your shirt."

"Not the first time," he said with a chuckle. Growing serious, he rubbed the small of her back. "Are you okay?"

"Yeah, it's just been an emotional month or so, to say the least." She turned to him, her faint smile drawing into a thin line. "Did you know Darla Mae had a half-brother?"

"Wow, that was quite the subject change." Grayson shook his head. "What are you talking about? Darla Mae was an only child."

"No, she wasn't," she told him. "Her father was married before Darla Mae's mother, and they had a son."

"That's not right," he said, sounding less convinced then he'd intended. "I would know if she had a brother." Wouldn't he?

"It's true," she said defiantly. "Obviously, Darla Mae is better at keeping secrets than you know."

"What does that mean?" he asked her, surprised by the cautious tone in his voice.

"Nothing," she stood up, her face red. "Forget I said anything."

When she turned to walk away, he stood up and reached for her arm. "Lexie, wait."

She jerked her arm back causing her to lose her footing on the rocks. She flailed her arms, trying to grab hold of something to break her fall. Grayson reached out to catch her. Unable to keep his balance, the two of them splashed into the cold river together.

Grayson sat up in the shallow water, and wiped his wet hair back from his eyes. He looked over at Lexie, who sat sputtering beside him. Her expression was a combination of shock and embarrassment until she met his eyes. A small giggle escaped from her throat and before long she was holding her stomach, laughing so hard she had tears streaming down her face.

"I can't believe you pulled me in with you," he said, splashing her. "You did that on purpose." He tried to sound serious, but her laughter was contagious, and he found himself laughing as hard as she was.

His laughter died away when he noticed she was bleeding. Instinctively he reached over to her and lifted her shirtsleeve to see where she was hurt.

"It's only a scratch, Grayson," she told him still smiling. "I'm in much better shape than your cell phone." She lifted what used to be his cell phone from the water. "I think this broke your fall," she added, stifling another giggle.

"I should've just stepped aside and let you fall in without helping you. It would serve you right for throwing a temper tantrum." He told her in a stern tone, but the twitching corners of his mouth made it impossible for him to appear serious.

"Temper tantrum?" she said incredulously. "I was not throwing a tantrum of any sort. I simply lost my balance." She turned her face away and dramatically stuck her nose into the air.

"What would you call this?" he asked her, tapping his finger on her nose. "This looks like another version of a tantrum to me."

She whipped around, catching him off guard and drenching him with a wave of water. He retaliated with another splash and leaned over her, threatening to hold her beneath the water if she didn't behave.

"Okay, okay, you win," she said, her wrists still tightly bound by his hands.

He lowered her arms and gradually let her go. "Now hold still and let me see this scratch of yours." He instructed lifting her sleeve again.

She was right, it was only a small scratch. Without thinking he bent over and gently placed a kiss on her cut arm. Realizing what he'd done, he lifted his head and raised his eyes. She wanted him to kiss her, he saw it in her eyes, in the breath she slowly pulled into her mouth, and the slight lean of her body toward his.

Her shirt was white, now transparent from the water. He leaned toward her, and took her mouth with the force of a man possessed. His hands gently caressed her breasts through the thin wet fabric. Her soft moan spurred him on as he dug his other hand into her hair and pulled her closer.

A loud splash behind them broke the spell and had them both scrambling to their feet. Neither of them could see the cause of the sudden splash, but both of them hurried from the water avoiding eye contact with each other.

As they silently turned to leave, Grayson spotted Darla Mae's retreating back through the trees.

Chapter 41

Lexie tossed and turned, struggling to fall asleep. Her body was crying out for Grayson, and her mind kept replaying their kiss. She almost believed he still loved her and that there was a chance for them after all. She'd finally realized how much she wanted to belong to him, to share her life, her son…his son.

Looking over at Ryan sleeping soundly beside her, she kissed his forehead and pulled the blankets over his shoulder. If she didn't stop rolling around she was sure she'd easily wake him. Slipping soundlessly from the bed, she pulled on her robe and let herself out of the room, easing the door closed behind her.

Walking quietly into the kitchen, she turned on the burner and set the kettle to boil. She hoped a nice hot cup of tea would relax her and allow her to rest. Using only the soft glow from the light above the stove, she set out a mug and dropped in a tea bag.

"You couldn't sleep either?"

She jumped and turned to see Grayson behind her. Instinctively she laid her palm on her chest as if to stop her racing heart. "You startled me," she managed to utter.

Shirtless, wearing only a low riding pair of pajama bottoms, she decided it was best to leave her hand where it rested on her chest. The urge to run her hands along the crests and valleys of his hard chest was strong. If this afternoon hadn't been enough, trying to sleep with this vision racing through her head would be impossible.

"I'm sorry," he said, his eyes twinkling with amusement. He smiled slyly, making it clear he'd noticed her survey of his body. "I couldn't sleep so I decided a midnight snack was in order."

Licking his lips, he stepped closer to her, his breath warm against her neck as he leaned in. It dawned on her that he hadn't been referring to food when he'd mentioned his craving for a midnight snack.

Her body hummed in anticipation, and her lips parted, welcoming his kiss. The heat from his body flooded through her thin robe, sending her blood boiling. The scent of him, the feel of him, was causing her to forget everything around her. Deciding he was taking too long, she reached her hands up and dug them into his hair, pulling his lips to hers.

Diving in, she felt herself drowning, her body bowing toward his with a mind of its own. He brought his arms around her and lifted her onto the kitchen island behind them. He stood between her legs, his mouth still busy exploring hers as he slipped her robe down from her shoulders.

Pulling his mouth from hers he kissed a soft trail down the side of her neck and along her collarbone; taking his time, he traced a path along her shoulder and down toward the swell of her breast. Her head fell back in painful ecstasy as her hips lifted, attempting to make contact with his.

She moaned his name as her body ignited into flames beneath his hands. Unable to stand the sweet agony any longer she reached for the tie to his pants in frantic desperation.

Locking eyes with him, she shifted closer. The ear splitting sound of the teakettle's whistle roared through the room causing them both to spring back in surprise.

Grayson walked over to the stove and lifted the kettle from the burner, silencing its shrill screech. Lexie pulled her robe onto her shoulders and slid from the counter. She could feel the flush in her cheeks and the need still lingering in her body, but now, she felt the unabridged distance between them as well.

He stood watching her, but saying nothing. The silence was thick, but neither of them seemed to know what to say. Twice in one day they'd been drawn together in passion, both times they were interrupted by a force she couldn't understand. She was beginning to wonder if the fates were trying to tell her something.

Grayson finally broke the silence. "I'm sorry," he said. His words cutting through her heart like a blade. "You're hard to resist, Lexie." He ran a hand through his hair, a gesture she knew he did in frustration. "I can't help it, I still want you, but…" he took a deep breath. "But we both know it will never work out between us…"

"So?" she prompted, her voice ringing with irritation.

"So, I have no right to toss you onto the kitchen counter, or kiss you, or hold you." In the dim light, she thought she saw his eyes fill with tears. "For that I'm sorry."

As she watched him walk from the kitchen, she thought about what he'd said. He'd sounded sorrier for feeling he had no right to her then for the fact they kept pulling toward each other like moths to a flame. She knew it was more than him still wanting her. He still loved her, regardless of the things she'd done. But being a man that knew what he wanted, Grayson would never get past what he considered to be her betrayal.

Filled with sadness, she sat in the silence and sipped her tea. She'd really blown it this time. Her suspicious, mistrusting nature had cost her the future she'd dreamed of, but never believed existed until she'd met Grayson.

Wiping her eyes, she slipped her mug into the dishwasher and quietly walked up the steps to her room. Hearing a creak in the floor, she stepped into the shadows along the hall and watched as Darla Mae slipped into Grayson's bedroom, wearing only a sheer black negligee.

She clenched her jaw, and balled her fists, holding tightly to her anger. It was easier than giving in to the hurt threatening to surface. Counting to fifty, she stepped into the light and let herself into her room.

Ryan was still sleeping soundly. She wasn't sure how she was going to sleep now, her traitorous mind shooting images of Grayson wrapped around Darla Mae the way he'd been wrapped around her only minutes ago.

Her stomach clenched, her heart ached, and she wanted to punch something. Anything would do, but if she could actually punch Darla Mae, she knew she'd feel even better.

Stamping down the annoying voice in her head screaming that she shouldn't do this, she stood up, straightened her back, and marched to the door. She'd sworn to herself she wouldn't let that malicious Barbie doll get her claws into Grayson, and she'd damned if she was going to sit here licking her wounds while she tried.

She'd just opened the door when she heard a shout. She watched as Darla Mae, head down, rushed from Grayson's room. His angry shouts cut off by the slamming of his door.

With a satisfied smile, Lexie closed her door and climbed back into bed beside her son. She was asleep the minute her head hit the pillow.

Chapter 42

Breakfast had been stressful. Lexie didn't think it was possible for anyone to be as negative as Lydia Hunter chose to be. She'd had enough of the woman's constant insults and references to DNA testing. Lydia had come up with a new possible conspiracy over fresh blueberry pancakes this morning. It seemed she believed Lexie was chasing Grayson for his money, as had Maggie—or Margaret, as Lydia referred to her. Truth be told, she wasn't chasing Grayson, and after close to a week with his mother, she was pretty sure that if they were together, his mother and their money could be a deal breaker.

Ryan had gone for another horseback ride with Grayson and William after breakfast, and she'd brought a hot cup of coffee to her favorite rocker on the side porch. She knew it was time for her to go home and relieve her mother at the coffee shop. After last night, she no longer worried about Darla Mae becoming Ryan's evil stepmother, and she knew Ryan would be fine without her.

It bothered her that she hadn't been able to figure out what had happened with Maggie. She was no closer to discovering who'd told her Grayson died, or why she'd never told the Hunters about Ryan. She was also still curious what Darla Mae's cryptic phone call was about, and the truth behind the secret half-brother, but realized that was more nosiness than anything else. Truth be told, she disliked the girl, and she was petty enough to just want dirt on her.

She frowned when Lydia appeared and made herself comfortable in the rocker beside her. So much for a nice quiet moment to herself.

Never one to beat around the bush, Lydia got straight to the point. "Are you going to give me a hard time regarding Ryan's necessary DNA test?"

Lexie didn't even bother to look at her. "No, I'm not. I understand how someone like you would require it."

Lydia's voice rose a notch, her sensibilities somehow insulted. "And what exactly do you mean, 'someone like me?'"

Shaking her head, she prayed Lydia would just walk away. Lexie hadn't yet calmed down from breakfast. The last thing she needed was for Lydia to gnaw through the final nerve, and for her to tell the hateful woman exactly what she meant.

"Nothing," she managed.

"My son stands to lose everything if he's wrong in trusting that…that…that dancer." Lydia spat.

Lexie's eyes narrowed and heat flooded her cheeks. She turned and stared at Lydia, fighting for control. She wanted to slap her. She wanted to slap her so hard that her head whipped to the side and her perfectly styled bun came uncoiled. "That dancer's name was Maggie. She was my friend, and a better woman than you could ever hope to be. She was also the mother of your grandchild, whether you like it or not, and she gave her life for his. I believe a little respect is due her," Lexie snarled.

Lydia looked surprised and a little ruffled, but continued in her haughty tone. "You mean my alleged grandson. That has not yet been proven."

Lexie bit down on her bottom lip. "You can call him whatever you like. And I will grant permission for Ryan to have the DNA test, so if that's all…"

Leaning forward, Lydia narrowed her eyes, and pursed her lips. "You do know that if it turns out Ryan is actually Grayson's son, there will be strict guidelines in place to protect Ryan, and Grayson. As the adoptive parent, you will not be allowed access to his trust."

Lexie clenched the arms of her chair until her knuckles were white. She pulled air into her lungs and let it out slowly. It didn't work. Pushing off from her chair, she stood in front of Lydia with her fisted hands on her hips. She could feel the heat in her face, and knew by Lydia's reaction she could see her anger.

"Now you listen to me," Lexie growled. "I don't want your damn money, and neither does my son. In fact, do me a favor, when the results come back, and you have the proof you require to know he's your grandson, be happy for Grayson, but stay away from my son."

"How dare you," Lydia's voice croaked.

Lexie glared at her, not backing down, all of her control snapped. "I can put up with your insults and your attempts to belittle me. But I will not stand by and let you insult my friend, or my son. Ryan has a grandmother and you're not good enough to share the same title with her. You are a bitter, lonely woman who can only stand tall when it's on the backs of others. You've alienated your husband and your son—"

"You have no right to speak me this way!" Lydia interrupted, standing up. Her face was drained of all color, and her hands were shaking as she pointed a finger at Lexie. "Just who do you think you are?"

"I'm no one, as you have so often pointed out. But the truth is, I'm on to you. I finally figured out why you're so rotten to me and why you were so rotten to Maggie." Lexie couldn't help but notice the insecurities flashing through Lydia's sad blue eyes. "You're jealous. Your son thinks you're cold and unfeeling and you know he's right. But when he cares for someone else, it radiates from him and you hate it. It's something you'll never have because you're unable to give it in return." She shook her head. "I pity you, Lydia. You're a miserable person with nothing but your money for company."

Lydia began to cry, her bottom lip quivering, as she stood there wringing her hands. Lexie wasn't sorry for what she'd said. She was sorry for Grayson, and William, and now for Ryan, but she was still too angry to feel bad for Lydia.

"Your son is an incredible man who hurt for a long time when he lost Maggie. He's lost her again only now, it's forever.

Try to remember that when you insult her in front of him. He's also discovered he has a son, but with that comes the knowledge that he's missed a huge part of his son's childhood that he can't get back. Get your damn DNA test, and try to be happy for him." She turned to leave, but stopped and faced Lydia again. "And I'd like to ask one favor of you. Please leave my son out of anything to do with Hunter money. I want him to be happy without believing that everyone in his life wants something from him."

*

Grayson heard the raised voices, and walked over in time to see Lexie stomp off, leaving his mother on the porch in tears. He stopped. His mother in tears? In his thirty years he couldn't recall a time he'd ever seen her cry.

"Mother, what is it, what's wrong?" He asked, racing up the stairs.

She appeared unable to speak, her body wracked with sobs. Crouching down in front of her, he was unsure of what to do. With any other crying woman he'd hold them, rock them, tell them it was going to be all right, but as his hands hovered over her, he realized he'd never hugged his mother before and wasn't sure how she would react if he did so now.

To his complete surprise, she leaned forward and hugged him, her face pressed to the nook between his neck and shoulders as she cried, and repeated "I'm sorry" over and over again.

Grayson didn't know what to say or how to react. It felt foreign to him, holding her, rubbing her back, comforting her. He finally managed, "Mother, what happened? Why are you so upset?"

Sitting up, she took a couple of deep hitching breathes, struggling to speak. "Lexie…she…said some things…"

He frowned and drew his brows together. "What things?"

"That I was cold, jealous, and a terrible mother." She began to cry again.

Grayson stood up, suddenly angry that Lexie would hurt his mother this way. "I'm sorry she spoke to you that way. She shouldn't have. I'll speak to her," he said, frustration evident in his tone.

He turned to leave.

"Grayson, wait," his mother called out.

He stopped and turned back around.

"She was right," his mother said softly. "About all of it."

Grayson's mouth hung open in amazement for a moment before he snapped it closed. "What?" he asked suspiciously.

His mother laughed. A genuine sound that had him wondering if he'd just entered the twilight zone.

"She's a smart girl. Mouthy and short fused, but smart."

"Lexie?" Grayson stuttered. "I mean, I know she's smart," he shrugged his shoulders, "and mouthy, and difficult, and stubborn, and untrusting, and—"

"Grayson," his mother smiled, "if you look deeply enough, you'll realize those are some of the reasons you love her."

Now he knew he was in another dimension or time. Either that or he was on some strange new candid camera or punked show.

"Mother, what has gotten into you? First you're crying, which never happens, second you hug me, which again, is not normal, but now…now you're in some strange way giving me relationship advice?" Grayson sat down in the rocker beside her, his eyes staring blindly into the afternoon sun.

Her voice grew faint, pained, and somehow genuine. "I'm sorry Grayson, for everything. For not trusting your judgment when it came to your heart, for not opening up to you so you could know how much I do care for you." She lowered her head, tearing her eyes away from his. "For not opening my arms to your son," she sniffled. "And for not being kind to Maggie, or to Lexie."

He watched her, struggling to recognize the woman in front of him as his mother. She raised her tear-stained eyes to his.

"I'm sorry about the years you've lost with Ryan," she said, reaching out and taking hold of his hand against the armrest.

He sat in silence, a million thoughts racing through his mind as he tried to take in everything she'd said to him.

"I'd like to start over, you and me. If that's something you believe is possible," she said sounding needy and insecure.

He placed his other hand over hers. "I'd like that very much."

The sat in silence for a while, both of them lost in their own thoughts. He watched her, rocking slowly with a smile of content on her face. He hated to do it, but he had to know and he knew there'd never be a time he'd get a more truthful answer from his mother.

"Mother, did you know Maggie was pregnant?"

Turning to him, he was surprised by the amount of genuine understanding in her eyes. "No, Grayson, I didn't, but I wish I had. I can't help but wonder if I wouldn't have been so unkind to her, would she have felt comfortable coming to us. Maybe if she had, you wouldn't have missed such valuable time with him."

He nodded, relieved she hadn't known and touched by her honesty.

"Thank you for your forgiveness, Grayson." She rose from her chair to leave. "Maybe you should find it in your heart to forgive someone else you love as well." With that, she turned and walked away.

Chapter 43

Lexie closed her eyes and breathed in the comforting scent of pine, moss, and wildflowers. She could hear the birds in the tree above her and opened her eyes to watch a squirrel shimmy up the trunk of a nearby tree. After her "chat" with Lydia, well not a chat per say, more like a cleansing, she'd taken a walk to clear her head.

She'd slipped into a grove of trees toward the back of the property and settled down in the grass beneath a large oak tree. What she needed was a little quiet. A little time to think, to process the information she did have and try to figure out a way to find the answers to the questions still nagging her.

Why had Maggie kept Grayson's family a secret from her? She could honestly say she hadn't asked about his family when they were discussing Ryan, but she'd assumed they didn't exist when they hadn't been mentioned.

Maggie was a huge family advocate, having lost her own at a young age. That was the part that made it harder to understand. Having met Lydia, she could understand Maggie wanting a bit of distance from her, but William was wonderful and seemed to have genuinely liked Maggie. That, combined with the fear of Ryan going into the system…It just didn't make sense.

Or had she been so hurt when she'd learned of Grayson's death that she couldn't be reminded of him? No, that couldn't be it either. Maggie would never put any selfish emotion over Ryan and family, of that she was sure. She wondered what Maggie would think of her and Grayson. Would she be happy for them? Would she feel betrayed? She smiled to herself, no, she would be glad they were together. She'd be happy that Grayson found someone, and that he'd found his son. Maggie would also be angry at the both of them for the mess they'd made of things.

Lexie reached over and picked a wild daisy growing in a bunch in front of her. Thinking about Grayson, their situation, his loss of Maggie, and wondering about her place in all this, she plucked one of the petals and let it fall to the ground. "He loves me," she said. Picking another petal she continued, "He loves me not." She pulled another, "He loves me…" Hearing the snap of twigs, she stood up preparing herself to run if she came across a wild animal of some sort. Instead, she saw the flash of blonde hair walking through the trees. It wasn't possible, Darla Mae, walking through the woods? The girl never ceased to surprise her.

Lexie let her walk ahead but made sure she could still see her before she slowly followed behind her. She quickly stepped behind a tree when Darla Mae's cell phone rang and she stopped to answer it.

Her voice sounded exasperated. "I did. He threw me out. Do you know how embarrassing that was for me?"

Lexie peeked around the tree and saw Darla Mae run a hand through her hair, and bend her head in what appeared to be defeat.

"He said it would never happen; that I was like his sister. That was after he called me Lexie." She snapped. "I threw myself at him and he was hoping I was someone else."

She was talking about last night with Grayson. Lexie felt a warmth spread through her. He'd wanted her to come to him.

"What?" Darla Mae shrieked into the phone. "Please don't ask me to do that. There has to be another way." She grew silent again. "Yes, I have it hidden. I was on my way to make sure it was safe when you called."

Now what was she talking about, Lexie wondered.

"That's easy for you to say. You're not the one seducing someone old enough to be your father. This isn't fair, there has to be another way," she said again.

Seducing an older man? Grayson was only a few years older than Darla Mae, so who was she talking about?

"I'm sure. He's so excited about this brat, he'll be furious with her when he finds it." She drew in a breath. "Okay, I get it. Consider it done."

Lexie stayed hidden as Darla Mae clicked her phone closed and headed deeper into the trees. Again, she tiptoed behind her, carefully avoiding any twigs or branches that could give her away. Where was she going?

Darla Mae stopped, forcing Lexie to jump behind a fallen log and lay silently on the ground. Darla Mae stood still, looking nervously over her shoulders and turning around to be sure no one was behind her. Lexie realized she'd landed in the perfect location to watch Darla Mae and avoid the chance of being discovered. She tried not to think about how foolish she must look laying behind a dead tree in the woods spying on a pampered southern princess.

Darla Mae crouched down and reached into a large knothole on the side of a tree. She pulled out a rusty metal box, wiped off the top and set it on her lap before opening it. From her hiding place she couldn't make out what was inside, but the smirk on Darla's Mae's face told her that whatever she'd been "checking on" was still safe.

Darla Mae slipped the box back into the knot of the tree, looked around one last time, and walked back the way she'd come. Lexie lay still until she was sure Darla Mae would've had time to leave the wooded area. She walked over to the tree and removed the box. Sitting down at the base of the tree, she slowly opened it.

Inside were stacks of letters. The top letter was addressed to William and Lydia from Maggie. Lexie's heart lurched and her hands shook as she pulled the letter from the envelope and stared at the newborn picture of Ryan.

> *Mr. and Mrs. Hunter,*
> *I want to start by telling you how sorry I am for your loss, and that I was unable to tell you personally when I came to see you. I'm sorry you felt my presence at the funeral would be too painful, but I wanted you to know I thought of you both that day, and pray your grief has eased, if only*

slightly. I received your letter and I was surprised to learn you didn't want to be a part of our child's life. I've tried to respect your wishes, but after looking into Ryan's face and seeing so much of Grayson, I wanted to reach out one last time. We have relocated to a small town in California and I have included our address. I hope we hear from you.

Margaret

Lexie read the letter again, trying to understand what she was reading. It sounded to her that it was the Hunters who told Maggie that Grayson had died. William had been so insistent that he hadn't seen her since she'd visited them with Grayson. She'd told them about Ryan, it was right here in black and white. She pulled the next letter from the box and saw that it was also from Maggie.

Mr. and Mrs. Hunter,

I understand from your lack of response to my previous letters that you have decided not to pursue a relationship with your grandson. As much as this hurts my heart, I respected your wishes. But things have changed and forced me to reach out to you one more time. I'm sick, dying actually, and that will leave Ryan alone. The thought of him being placed in the system with the possibility of being moved from home to home with no stability scares me. This is the biggest thing I've ever asked of anyone, but could you find it in your heart to open your lives to this innocent little boy? You're all the family he will have left and he deserves to live a full happy life filled with love. I'm not sure how much time I have left, so please understand the importance of making this decision as quickly as possible.

Margaret

Tears streamed down Lexie's cheeks as she read the desperation in her friend's request. Had they received this letter and chose to turn their backs on Ryan? That would devastate Grayson. Why had she followed Darla Mae? What was she supposed to do with this information? Arching her brows, it suddenly dawned on her—Darla Mae had these letters hidden inside a tree. Had it been her all along who kept Grayson from his son? If so, why?

She pulled out the next letter, addressed to Grayson and marked personal, but without an address. It had been opened, and Lexie felt uneasy as she unfolded the soft pink paper.

> *My dearest Grayson,*
>
> *I know I have no right to contact you after leaving you the way I did. I'm sorry for any pain I've caused you. Please know it was the hardest thing I've ever done and I had the best of intentions with my decision to set you free, although knowing you the way I do, you will disagree with me. Shortly before your deployment, they told me I have cancer. Loving you the way I do, I couldn't risk your safety if you were distracted with worry over me. I can hear you now, shouting what I fool I am and how selfish I was to make that decision for you. I'm right, aren't I, that's exactly what you did. I need you to stop being angry and focus on what I have to tell you next. Baby, we're pregnant. I swear I didn't know at the time, but now that I do, I'm over the moon with the happiness of it. I don't want to be without you, and I want us to be a family. Please forgive me for letting you go, and come home to us safely. I don't know how to reach you, but I'm going to drop in on your family to share our news, and I will have them send this letter to you. Please contact me at the address below. I pray for you every minute of every day and can't wait to hold you and lay our baby safely in your arms.*

All my love,
Maggie

Grayson had never received this letter. Anger surged through her as she remembered Maggie laying Ryan in her arms instead of his father's. Four years of Ryan's life would have no memories of his father, and his father would have no memories of him. Spurred on by her anger, she dipped inside the box and realized the remaining letters were from Grayson to Maggie.

In the same way her letter had been without an address, so were his. It was becoming clear to her that they had relied on his parents to forward the mail to each other. Her only question now was how much did William and Lydia know, or—like Maggie and Grayson—were they victims of Darla Mae also?

Most importantly, exactly what was Darla Mae up to?

Chapter 44

Lexie walked in through the back door with the metal box tucked under her arm. She wasn't exactly sure how to handle the situation her nosiness had gotten her into, but she knew it would involve sitting the Hunters down together for a clear understanding of the events between Grayson's deployment and Maggie's death.

But first, she needed a shower, and to check on her son. Then, she was going to confront Darla Mae.

She wound up the stairs, her head reeling with unanswered questions. An angry growl behind her snapped her back from her reverie.

"Where did you get that?" Darla Mae barked, her lips curled back in a snarl. "Give that back."

Lexie shook her head in disgust.

"Did you follow me?" Darla Mae snapped.

Choosing to ignore her question, Lexie asked one of her own. "Who were you talking to on the phone? Who's in on this with you?"

Shock registered in her expression before she buried it with her false sarcastic smile. "I have no idea what you're talking about."

"I wonder if William and Lydia would know. I'll just wait and ask them," Lexie said, stepping around her.

Darla Mae tackled her from behind, sending them both tumbling onto the hallway carpet. Lexie gripped the box tightly against her chest, while Darla Mae tried to rip it from her arms.

"What's in this for you, Darla Mae? Revenge? Some weird twisted feelings you harbor for Grayson? What makes somebody go to so much trouble to keep a couple apart?" Lexie asked her all the while keeping a tight grip on the box.

Darla Mae managed to get Lexie onto her back and straddled her to hold her there. "Give me the damn box, Lexie. I mean it!"

"No," Lexie told her calmly.

"You meddling bitch. You don't know who you're messing with." Her normally milky white face was now blood red with rage. "My brother—"

Darla Mae tried to stop herself, but Lexie was now sure who'd been on the other end of the phone. "I thought so," she said arrogantly. She saw the surprise on Darla's face, and pushed for more information, baiting her. "You think I didn't know you had a half-brother? I know a lot about you, Darla Mae."

"Well, good, then I don't have to waste my time explaining the small details to you," she sneered. "This family owes us. My brother and I just want what's ours."

Lexie wanted to keep her talking, but knew she had to keep hold of the box at all costs. "What exactly do you believe is yours? Grayson?"

"I don't give a damn about Grayson, I just want the money that's owed to me and he was a means to an end." Darla Mae flexed her lips dismissively. "He never knew what was good for him anyhow. Falling all over himself for stupid, worthless girls who would never appreciate him."

"Like you do?" Lexie baited her.

"I appreciate him in my own way, yes." Darla Mae leaned down bringing her face inches from Lexie's. "That silly brainless dancer hit the jackpot though. She got herself knocked up with a belly full of cash. I fixed that," she said through clenched teeth. "Then you show up, with the brat in tow, and Grayson foaming at the mouth over you."

"You planned on keeping his child a secret and then what, having one of your own?" Lexie asked with disgust.

"She said it was his kid, but hell, it could have been anyone's."

Lexie felt her stomach clench and her hands ball up as she struggled to keep the box in a tight grip. "You knew it was his, or you wouldn't have gone to all this trouble to keep it from him," she said logically.

"She dumped him; she didn't deserve a second chance."

"That must have pissed you off," Lexie continued. "She had the man you wanted wrapped around her finger and she just dumped him."

"She didn't deserve him." Darla Mae seemed to relax a little. "Then she shows up here trying to find him, to share the 'good news.' I'll be damned if I let that little tramp ruin everything I'd worked so hard for."

Darla Mae no longer realized they were lying in the middle of the hallway floor. Her eyes were glassy and distant and more than a bit crazed.

"So you told her that Grayson had died," Lexie stated rather than asked.

"She dropped the letter she was holding, turned on her heels and walked away, just like that," Darla Mae said with revulsion. "Then she shows up here the following day wanting to pay her respects to his parents. Give me a break, like they'd want to see her even if he was dead," she snorted.

All the pieces were beginning to fall into place. "So you told her they didn't want to see her and sent her on her way again."

Lexie didn't think Darla Mae even remembered who she was talking to as she continued on with her wild story.

"Then she sends a letter telling them about the baby and I responded to her telling her we don't want anything to do with it."

"You responded for them?" Lexie asked, trying to keep her disdain from coming through in her tone.

"Yeah, they had enough to worry about with Grayson getting shot in Iraq. They didn't need some money grubber coming around," she justified. "Then she sends another letter with a picture; have mercy, what did it take to get through to this girl?" She shook her head. "I had to race to check the mail every day for over a year to keep her letters from them and Grayson's from her. It was exhausting, but necessary."

"Why do they owe you, Darla Mae? What did they do to you?" Lexie asked trying to sound sympathetic.

Darla Mae seemed to snap out of her trance, and glared at Lexie with hate-filled eyes. "They took everything from me." She reached for the box and tried to pry Lexie's fingers away. "I won't let you ruin this, now give me the damn box," she screamed.

"It's too late, Darla Mae," Lexie said trying to sound confident. "The jig is up, shall we say."

Darla Mae grew angrier and more insistent on taking the box from her. She shrieked and fought, leaving fingernail scratches along Lexie's chest and arms, but she wasn't letting go.

Grayson raced up the stairs, obviously hearing Darla Mae's shouting. He paused, seeming shocked by the scene in the hallway.

"Get her off me," Lexie yelled.

With what appeared to be no effort at all, Grayson lifted Darla Mae off her and set her feet onto the floor before helping Lexie up.

"What the hell is going on here?" Grayson asked sharply.

Lexie turned to him, "Nothing, can you wait for me downstairs? I need to talk to you."

He stared at her mutely for a minute, and then at Darla Mae. He seemed concerned, and more than a little confused, but with a small nod of his head, he walked back down the stairs.

Lexie turned to Darla Mae. "I recommend you get your things together quickly. For your own safety you will want to be gone before Grayson finds out what you've done."

With those final words, she marched into her room and shut the door behind her.

Chapter 45

Lexie showered with the bathroom door locked and the box sitting within arm's reach outside the shower door. She'd needed a minute to gather her thoughts, but after standing under the steaming hot water for close to twenty minutes, she still had no idea where to begin when she spoke to Grayson and his parents.

She slipped into her favorite pair of jeans and a t-shirt, threw on a light sweater and a comfortable pair of flats. Tonight, she didn't care what Lydia thought of how she dressed. This was her and Lydia would just have to deal with it. Besides, after their talk she couldn't imagine Lydia would remember or care what she'd been wearing.

She pulled her wet hair around and braided it, letting it fall down over her right shoulder. Taking a minute to study herself in the mirror, she took a deep breath, picked up the metal box and walked from the room. This time she looked over her shoulder repeatedly, making sure nobody was in waiting to jump her from behind. Once had been enough for her.

She found Grayson and his father in one of the cozy sitting rooms, each sipping from a brandy snifter. They both looked up at her anxiously when she walked into the room. It was obvious Grayson had told his father about the scuffle he'd broken up between her and Darla Mae.

"Lexie, are you okay?" Grayson asked her, rising from the sofa and walking to her.

"I'm fine," she answered. "Will you two wait here for me? I need to talk to you both."

"Of course," William said, his eyes squinting curiously.

"I'll be right back." Without releasing her grip on the box, she walked from the room to check on Ryan and to find Lydia.

Hearing Ryan's laughter from the kitchen, she walked down the hall and through the swinging door. She froze, her mouth dropping open in astonishment. Ryan was sitting at the kitchen table with Lydia, playing a game of Go Fish.

Lydia looked up at her and gave her a warm smile. "He's good at this game, I don't think I stand a chance of winning against him," she said.

"Grandma learned fast," Ryan told her before asking Lydia for a seven and grinning widely when she handed him two and called him a little stinker.

Had Ryan really just called her grandma? Had she imagined the previous week, or was she imagining now? She closed her eyes and shook her head as if to clear her sight. No, she wasn't imagining things. She'd opened her eyes to the same scene she'd witnessed before she'd closed them.

"Were you looking for Ryan?" Lydia asked her.

Lexie had to stop and think about her question for a moment. "Um yes, and you too," she said, sounding unsure even to herself. "I needed to talk to you and thought maybe Ryan would like to go help Billy feed the horses."

Ryan grinned from ear to ear, set his cards on the table face up and raced from his chair to get his "pointy boots" on. Lexie stopped and studied Lydia's expression, surprised by the amount of joy she saw. Who was this woman, and what had she done with Lydia?

"I'm glad you're here, I wanted to speak to you also," Lydia said, coming around the table. "I wanted to thank you for what you did."

Lexie eyed her suspiciously. "What I did?"

Lydia nodded her head. "For being honest with me. For making me see how many blessings I'd been overlooking, and for raising my grandson." Her eyes filled with tears. "He's a wonderful, happy little boy."

Lexie, needing to sit down, pulled out Ryan's abandoned chair and began to drink his warm milk. His half-full glass was sitting next to an almost empty plate of cookies. "Are those chocolate chip cookies?"

Lydia actually blushed. "They are. I've never baked anything in my life, but Ryan is a great teacher."

Lexie gasped. "You baked?" Her eyes grew wide. "With Ryan?"

Lydia smiled, seeming a little embarrassed. "I know, it's crazy don't you think?"

"Lydia, what is going on with you?" Lexie looked at her with her brows knit. "You're in the kitchen, playing Go Fish and baking cookies with my son, *and* he's calling you Grandma. I don't understand."

Lydia bowed her head for a moment, and when she looked up at Lexie, she had a sheen of tears in her eyes. "You were right—about everything. I have been cold, and very selfish. William reminded me of the way my parents had disapproved of him when I brought him home. He was a ranch hand and I was the only child in a very wealthy family. They expected me to marry up, to look at it as a business arrangement, not to fall in love with a man who worked in their barns. I don't know how I couldn't see that I was behaving in the exact same manner they had, or remember how it felt knowing they were so wrong. I swore I would never be like my mother and instead, I was worse. I've been unfair to my son, to my husband, and extremely unkind to you. But I want a fresh start, a chance to do things right with my grandson. I don't want to make the same mistakes."

Lexie didn't respond. She was amazed by what she was hearing.

"I lost my chance to apologize to Maggie, but I hope you will accept my very humble apology, and try to forgive the horrible things I've said. I'd very much like a chance to get to know you, and to be a part of Ryan's life."

Lexie was surprised when her own eyes filled with tears. "Of course, Lydia, I'd never keep you from Ryan, and I accept your apology. I hope you'll accept mine as well. I was out of line in the way I spoke to you earlier."

Lydia walked to her and placed her palm against Lexie's cheek. "You don't owe me an apology. You were right. In fact, I should thank you for the things you said. I needed to hear them. I've spent years believing I had to behave a certain way, maybe it was the way I was brought up, I don't know, but I don't want to be that woman. It won't be easy for me to change, especially at this stage of my life, but I want to try."

Lexie smiled at her, and attempted to lift her arm to wipe her eyes when she realized she was still clutching the box beneath her arm.

"Do you have a minute? I need to talk to all of you. William and Grayson are waiting in the sitting room."

Lydia nodded her head, her eyes curious, and followed her into the other room. Once everyone was seated, silently waiting for her to speak, she couldn't remember how she wanted to tell them, or what she would say. She stood there with her mouth open, like a sucker fish against a glass aquarium.

"Lexie, are you all right?" Grayson asked her, beginning to rise from his seat on the sofa.

She nodded her head and waved her hand instructing him to stay seated. "I don't know where to begin, so bear with me if I sound a bit crazy."

All three of them nodded and sat watching her with curiosity.

"I've been struggling to understand everything that happened after Grayson's deployment and prior to Maggie's death." She swallowed, and cleared her throat. "So much of it didn't make sense to me." She looked down at the box in her lap and ran her fingers over the dusty metal surface. "Through some snooping I'm not exactly proud of, I believe I finally have the pieces that have been missing."

Grayson leaned forward, confusion and relief each taking turns with his expression. "What pieces?" he asked.

William reached over and patted his son's knee. "Let her finish, son."

Lexie's eyes locked onto Grayson's. She wanted to tell him, to reassure him that they'd all been victims of a horrible scheme, but she knew he would have to mourn again. He would know Maggie tried to reach out to him and both of them were lied to. She knew her words would hurt him, and she wanted to protect him.

"Lexie, please…" he begged.

She had to tell him, she had no choice. He deserved the truth after all these years.

"It was Darla Mae. She was the one behind everything," she finally blurted out.

Lydia gasped and William looked at her like she'd lost her mind. But Grayson stood up, anger surging through him. "What do you mean?"

"When Maggie discovered she was pregnant, she came here." Lexie looked from William to Lydia. "She wanted to tell you both in person, and to find out how to reach Grayson. Instead, she ran into Darla Mae. She told Maggie that Grayson died in Iraq."

Lydia uncrossed her legs and straightened her back. "Why would Darla Mae do that?" she asked in a quiet voice.

"This is where it gets a little foggy," Lexie replied. "It seems Darla Mae and her half-brother concocted this scheme—"

"Wait a minute," William interrupted. "Darla Mae doesn't have a brother."

Lexie's voice softened when she saw the pain in his eyes. "Actually, she does, from her father's first marriage." When nobody replied, she continued. "They believe that you owe them financially. She admitted as much."

"We took her into our home, into our family." Lydia choked. "How could she think we owed her…?"

"Her father gambled their fortune away. Why would she think we were in any way responsible?" William asked.

"I think I know," Grayson said. He ran his hands over his face and took a deep breath. "Do you remember the last big derby the

Pruitt's entered? It was the race they were disqualified for using enhancement drugs on their horse."

"Of course I remember," William replied.

"That was the year Old Blue Bell took the title," Lydia added.

Grayson nodded his head. "Exactly, but did you know that it was me and Billy that turned the Pruitt's in?"

William and Lydia gasped. Lexie continued to put the pieces together as he spoke.

"Billy had heard they were drugging their horses, and that they had caused one's death. Billy doesn't deal well with abuse of any kind to the horses, you know that." Grayson said to his parents. "When he was preparing Old Blue Bell before the race, he saw Pruitt's trainer injecting their horse and sent me to get the authorities."

"I still don't understand how any of this comes back to our owing anything to Darla Mae," Lydia interjected.

"That was the race that Mr. Pruitt bet every penny they had and lost it all. It was only a few weeks later when they were killed in that accident. There was nothing left for Darla Mae or this mysterious brother to inherit," Grayson told them.

Lydia and William both looked up at each other obvious both of them had just thought of something. "There were a lot of questions regarding their accident," William said aloud.

Grayson appeared lost. "What questions?"

"Whether it was suicide or an accident," Lexie answered.

Lydia looked at her with awe. "You have been busy," she told her. "They were already selling the ranch and the animals to pay off the creditors and the bookies; we didn't want to see Darla Mae lose the life insurance as well. She wouldn't receive a dime if it was deemed suicide."

"So you made sure it stayed filed as an accident," Lexie filled in.

Grayson looked surprised by the information. "Okay, so you saved her the life insurance money, took her into our home, and raised her. Where in all of this does she come to the conclusion we owe her a damn thing?" he asked with frustration.

"It doesn't make a lot of sense, but it seemed to me that she blamed you for the loss of the ranch," Lexie told him. "She kept saying 'they took everything from me.'"

Grayson raised his voice. "Okay, so the bitch was crazy and thought she was somehow entitled to a large sum of money from us. What does that have to do with her telling Maggie I'd died? What reward was there in that?"

"Darla Mae's plan involved being with you, Grayson. She saw Maggie as a threat to that plan." Lexie noticed the disgusted look on Grayson's face. "She thought she was home free when Maggie broke things off before you deployed."

"But then she came back and tried to find me," Grayson said aloud, the pieces slowly sliding into place. "I understand that Maggie believed I was dead," Grayson added. "But why didn't she reach out to my parents when she realized she was pregnant?"

Lexie looked at him sympathetically. "She did."

Both William and Lydia looked panicked, shaking their heads wildly. "No, she didn't," they both said at once.

"I swear to you, son, we had no idea." Lydia yelped frantically.

"You didn't know," Lexie clarified, "but she did reach out to you."

"How do you know all of this?" William asked.

Lexie sat the metal case onto the table and opened the lid. "Darla Mae had this hidden in a tree on the back of the property. I followed her, that's how I found it."

Grayson looked inside the open box and pulled out the newborn picture of Ryan. Her heart broke for him as he pulled out the letter addressed to him from Maggie.

Lydia and William reached out and clasped each other's hands, both carefully watching their son as he sat silently reading with tears streaming down his cheeks.

Lexie watched them pull out one of the letters addressed to them and lean in to read it together. She turned and left the room quietly. She needed to find her son and get their bags packed. It was time to go home. The Hunters needed time together to mourn and heal.

After watching Grayson's face as he read Maggie's declaration of love, she knew she would need time to mourn as well. It was at that moment she realized she'd lost him for good.

Chapter 46

Lexie wiped down the counter, pulled out the inventory sheet she'd been working on, and wrote down the syrups she needed. She was trying desperately to keep herself busy.

In the two weeks since she'd been home, she jumped every time the phone rang, and worse, every time the bell over the door tinkled in her shop. There had been no word from Grayson. She hadn't expected to hear from him but a part of her had hoped she would.

She was growing tired of her own company. She was depressing, if she were to be honest. But everyone in her life was busy with other things. Ryan was still mad at her for making him leave the ranch early and taking him away from his "cowboy job." Marissa was working double shifts, filling in for a co-worker on maternity leave, and Jordan was working long hours due to Grayson's absence. She could have spent time with her mom, but the thought of her *tsk*-ing, and "how could you let him get away" speech was more than she was ready to handle.

The shop was closed, and she still had an hour to kill before her mother brought Ryan back from the newest Disney movie at the theater. She cranked up the stereo to drown out her own thoughts and danced around behind the counter, counting supplies to the rhythm of the music. "I'll be okay," she blared out with the song. And she would, damn it, she thought to herself. She'd been alone for a long time before Grayson Hunter came along. It would be easy to get back into her old routine.

She'd almost had herself convinced when she heard the tinkle of the bell and felt her heart drop. Okay, so it would take a bit of time. She could do it. She took a deep breath to calm herself and pasted a smile on her face for her son's benefit before turning around.

Her smile vanished, and she gasped in surprise when Ryan

walked through the door with Grayson by his side.

"Hi Mom," Ryan sang, his happiness at seeing Grayson radiating from him. "Grayson's back! He missed us." He skipped around the shop, and made his way into Lexie's office.

"So I see," she managed. Slowly raising her eyes to Grayson's, she managed only, "Hi."

He didn't smile; he simply watched her, saying nothing for a time. She felt uncomfortable beneath his steely gaze.

Damn him, she thought. It was just like him to show up when he was heavy on her mind, and worse, when she wasn't expecting him and looked like she'd been run over by a milk truck. Damn him again, for always looking so damn sexy. She knew she was in trouble when her inner go-to word was damn.

"Darla Mae left," he said.

Her head jerked up. "That's good," she said, surprised that after two weeks, this was the first thing he felt he needed to tell her. "I think, isn't it?"

"It is good," he smiled at her. "My parents are renewing their vows on New Year's Eve. I've never seen them happier."

She nodded her head. "I'm glad," she said quietly.

"It's because of you, you know that?" he told her.

"Because of me?" she asked, confused.

He chuckled. "I have no idea exactly what you said to my mother, but it's like an exorcism had been performed. She's a completely different person."

She smiled slyly. "You don't want me to repeat the things I said to your mother. It wasn't pretty."

"That much I do know," he laughed. "Remind me never to get on your bad side."

"It's best to avoid that side."

"I've missed you," he said watching her face intently.

Her smile faded, and her heart raced. She didn't know what to say, or what he was saying.

"I've said my final goodbyes to Maggie," he said, his eyes locked with hers. "Thank you for giving her back to me."

Lexie was sure she felt a small crack running through her heart. She fought back the tears and managed to nod her head.

"Will you excuse me for a minute," he asked her before walking into her office.

Only a second later, he came back out with Ryan. Her son had a huge grin on his face, and to her surprise, it matched Grayson's. Before she could ask why, both of them dropped to one knee on the floor in front of her. Grayson flipped open a small velvet box with a very large square solitaire diamond inside. Her eyes grew wide, and her hands flew to her chest.

"Will you marry us?" they said in unison.

Tears rolled down her cheeks and she looked at her two favorite men kneeling before her. "Are you sure?" she asked Grayson, still unsure if she was dreaming.

"I've never been more sure of anything in my life," he told her, getting to his feet. He pulled the ring from the box and slipped it onto her finger. It all but blinded her when she flashed it into the light. "I know it's rather large, but it was my mother's and she insisted that she wanted you to have it."

Lexie's head shot up. "Your mother insisted?"

Grayson laughed at her shocked expression. "Yes, she did. She's crazy about you. I swear I'll never understand women."

She laughed too. "You don't want to, we'd be far less interesting and you'd be bored with us."

His eyes grew serious. "You still haven't answered me, Lexie." He took her hand in his. "Will you marry me?"

"Grayson, I want to scream yes from the rooftops, but…"

"But what, Lexie?" Grayson stepped back, putting some space between them.

"You've just said your goodbyes to Maggie. I don't want to be the rebound girl, or second choice girl, or whatever. And I don't want you to feel you'll miss out on anything with Ryan if were not married," she said breathlessly.

Grayson shook his head and stepped closer to her again. "Lexie, I will always love Maggie. She was my first love and she gave me my son. But she also gave me you. She is my past, and you are my forever. You're not second choice, your my first and only choice." He lifted her chin, forcing her to look him in the eye. "When I thanked you for giving her back to me, it was because by showing me the truth, you gave me a part of myself back that I didn't know I'd been missing." Stepping away, he ran his hand through his hair and paced in front of her. He stopped and looked at her, his eyes searching hers. "I didn't think I was good enough for you. I'd given my all to someone who I believed had thrown it back in my face. So how could my best be enough? You deserve the best, Lexie, and I want to be that man for you."

Lexie threw herself into his arms, tears of joy streaming down her face. "Yes, yes, yes," she said, kissing him soundly on the mouth.

"Now?" Ryan asked, tugging on Grayson's pant leg.

Grayson looked down, smiled and nodded his head before turning to look at Lexie. "Don't be mad," he told her.

Before Lexie could ask him what about, a large golden puppy with feet the size of grapefruits bolted through the door heading straight for them, dragging Ryan behind him by a leash.

Grayson tried to reach for the puppy, causing him to switch paths. His leash, still connected to Ryan, wrapped around Lexie's legs, pulling them out from under her. Grayson raced to catch her, tripping over the leash, and pulling them both down in a heap on the floor.

The large puppy finally stopped his race, lay down with a plop beside them, and began to lick their faces.

"We really need to work on your coordination," he told her.

She slapped him playfully on the shoulder. She looked over at the puppy, now happily chewing his way through his leash. "Grayson, a dog, really?"

"It was that or a horse. I kind of thought you'd be less mad about a dog," he told her, his face a portrait of innocence.

"But Dad says he'll work on you to get me a horse by next spring," Ryan volunteered as he sat grinning at his new puppy.

"Oh, did he now?" Lexie looked at him with a wicked glint in her eye before laying her head onto the floor and pulling him down for a kiss.

"We really have to stop meeting like this," he said smiling deviously before losing himself in her kiss.

About the Author

Erin McCauley currently lives in the Pacific Northwest with her three children, and her dedicated writing partner, Maxx, her three-pound Yorkie. She enjoys writing about the bonds of family and the true strength of friendship, and the importance of both during our journeys to find love. She is currently working on Marissa and Jordan's journey, *The Betrayal*, coming May 2013.

Visit her at *www.erinmccauley.com*.

In the mood for more Crimson Romance? Check out *My Nora* by Holley Trent at *CrimsonRomance.com*.